I0679515

RETIRED ASSASSINS' CLUB, VOLUME 1

A COLLECTION OF SHORT SPY THRILLERS

SAM CHASE

Copyright © 2025 by Sam Chase
All rights reserved.
No part of this book may be reproduced in any form or by any electronic or
mechanical means, including information storage and retrieval systems, without
written permission from the author, except for the use of brief quotations in a book
review.

First Edition

Editing by Jessica McKenna
Cover by Sam Chase

BEACHES AND TRAILS
PUBLISHING

THE SCHOLAR

A SHORT THRILLER

CHAPTER 1
THE GLOBE COLLECTION

GABRIEL KANE HAD forty-one vintage globes.

He could tell you where each one came from, what it had cost, and — if he was being honest with himself, which he tried not to be before his first cup of tea — what he had been doing the week he found it. The one on the kitchen windowsill: a brass-mounted Bellerby from a market stall in Vienna, acquired two days after a job he didn't think about anymore. The pair of celestial spheres on the mantelpiece: bought in a single afternoon in Istanbul because the seller was a retired cartographer who could talk for hours about how explorers used to draw sea monsters in the blank spaces rather than admit they didn't know what was there.

There be dragons, the old cartographers wrote. Gabriel had always liked that. An honest admission of ignorance, dressed in mythology.

He wrapped the teapot in its cozy — hand-knitted green wool, embroidered with small golden globes in places he'd been, a gift from a previous version of himself who'd had more sentiment than sense — and carried his tea to the window. Below, the Alfama district was waking up in its unhurried way: trams groaning uphill, pigeons conducting their morning arguments, the smell of bread from the pastelaria two streets over.

He'd been here fourteen months. Long enough to know which café charged for the bread basket and which one didn't. Long enough to have a usual order at three different establishments and to be greeted by name at all of them. Long enough, he'd thought, to count as settled.

He looked at the street below and drank his tea and thought about nothing in particular, which was a skill he'd worked very hard to develop.

In precisely twenty-eight minutes, he would walk to the university and spend ninety minutes explaining to undergraduates that the Persian Wars were not, in fact, about heroism. They were about geography, economics, and the specific way that fear makes men overreach. The students in the front row would write this down. The students in the back row would type something unrelated on their phones. Gabriel had made peace with this distribution.

He retrieved his notes from the desk, pausing as he always did at the globe of the Indian subcontinent — a hand-coloured 1920s reproduction, slightly inaccurate in the way of its era, the borders drawn with the confidence of people who hadn't been there. He'd bought it in Bangalore, the week before Charlotte Hayes was taken. Before John Hayes became a different kind of man entirely.

Don't.

He moved his hand away from the globe and picked up his bag instead.

The sedan outside was new.

He noticed it the way he noticed most things that didn't belong: without appearing to, without breaking his routine, his eyes tracking the plates in a single pass as he shouldered the bag and locked the door. Portuguese plates, but the registration sequence was wrong for a vehicle this age. And it was parked where faculty weren't permitted to park, at an angle that gave a clean sightline to the door of the History building.

Someone's watching the building. Not me specifically.
He filed it and walked to work.

⁂

THE LECTURE WENT WELL. The front row took notes. The back row did not.

Afterward, Gabriel sat in his office with a cooling coffee and the student papers he was supposed to be marking. He marked three of them. He was very thorough.

On the fourth paper, he stopped.

He'd been doing this for twenty minutes: sitting with his pen in his hand while his mind worked on something else entirely. It was a historian's reflex — the inability to look at a collection of data without searching it for a pattern. His students found it impressive when he did it with primary sources. He found it inconvenient when he did it with his own life.

The sedan has been there since yesterday.

He knew because yesterday, walking back from the faculty car park, he'd noted the plates in passing — a minor anomaly he'd filed and not revisited. Now, filed alongside today's sighting, it resolved into something different.

Not watching the building. Watching the route.

He set the marking aside, stood, and went to the window. Third floor, north-facing, looked out over the car park and the street beyond. The sedan was gone.

He felt the particular absence of relief.

On his desk, beneath the stack of unmarked papers, his personal phone buzzed once.

One buzz. The pattern he'd coded for himself, years ago, for the dead-drop address he'd never cancelled because cancelling it would have required logging back into systems he preferred to pretend didn't know his name.

Someone just accessed the Scholar dead-drop.

He stood at the window for a moment longer, looking at the empty parking space.

Then he sat down, opened his laptop — the personal one, not the university machine — and navigated to an email account that had last been active fourteen months ago.

One message. No subject line. No sender name. Just a string of numbers that decoded, with a key he hadn't used since Vienna, into seven words.

Someone is running Scholar. It isn't you.

CHAPTER 2
PATTERN RECOGNITION

GABRIEL SPENT the evening at his kitchen table with three things: the decoded message, a glass of wine he wasn't drinking, and the specific kind of silence that happens when a historian puts primary sources in front of him that he doesn't want to interpret.

The message had come through a dead-drop he'd set up himself, in the first year of what he'd optimistically called retirement. An automated tripwire — any access to a dormant Agency file associated with the Scholar designation would trigger a notification to the encrypted address. He'd built it as an early warning system and then, when fourteen months had passed without a signal, had begun the slow process of convincing himself he didn't need one.

Someone is running Scholar. It isn't you.

He read it again.

He thought about the sedan. The wrong plates. The sightline to his door.

He got up and went to the globe of Eastern Europe — a mid-century political model, the borders already wrong before the ink had dried — and turned it slowly in his hands the way he did when he was thinking through a problem he didn't want to approach directly.

What does it mean for someone to run your designation?

It meant they had access to Agency infrastructure at the level of operational assignment. Not a breach, not a hack — this was internal. Someone within the current directorate had pulled the Scholar designation out of the archive, marked it active, and was using it to run an operation.

An operation Gabriel knew nothing about.

Which meant that somewhere, in a file that would eventually be audited, reviewed, or leaked, there was a paper trail that read: *Asset K-412-A — Scholar — operational. Current assignment:* whatever they'd decided he was doing.

And when that trail was followed — when an oversight body, an investigative journalist, or a foreign intelligence service pulled that thread — it would lead here. To this apartment. To this desk. To this man who had spent fourteen months building a life on the premise that nobody was looking.

Gabriel set the globe down.

They're not watching me because they're hunting me.

They're watching me because they need to know where I am.

He crossed to the window. The sedan was back. Parked differently this time — two streets over, new angle. Covering the secondary exit from the building.

Amateur. Or deliberate. The same thought he'd had in Lisbon the day the photograph arrived, fourteen months ago. The day he'd stopped being Gabriel Kane the history teacher for twenty-four hours and gone back to being something else.

He let the curtain fall.

There were two things he needed: the operational file, to understand what Scholar was supposedly doing. And a technical specialist, to access the Agency's current network without triggering the monitoring protocols that the new directorate had presumably installed after everything that had happened with Lyon.

He knew exactly who to call for the second.

He just needed to decide whether he wanted to.

CHAPTER 3
THE LOCKSMITH

THE COASTAL ROAD south of Lisbon ran through a sequence of small towns that were beautiful in the summer and forgotten in November, which is why people who wanted to be forgotten tended to arrive in November.

Ivan Petrov had arrived three years ago, in the grey of February, and had been so thoroughly forgotten that the entire local community had developed a warm and personal affection for him. He fixed their locks. He kept strange hours and stranger company. He carved wooden birds that he left on the counter for customers to take if they wanted one. He paid his taxes on time and never asked questions about anyone else's business, which in a small coastal town is the highest possible form of social grace.

Gabriel parked on the seafront and walked the rest of the way.

The shop's sign read *Petrov — Repairs and Restoration* in hand-painted letters that had faded to the colour of the sea on a grey day. A bell above the door announced him. Inside, the smell of machine oil and sawdust and something sharper underneath — a specific calibre of gun oil that Gabriel recognised without looking for it.

Ivan was at the workbench with a lock mechanism spread open before him like a small, intricate surgery. He didn't look up.

"Door was unlocked," Gabriel said.

"Door's always unlocked." Ivan held a component up to the light, examined it. "It's a locksmith shop. People need to be able to get in." He set the piece down and turned on his stool. A broad face. A beard that had grown in three years from stubble to something comfortable and substantial. Eyes that assessed and then relaxed into recognition, followed by the particular wariness of a man who had learned that visitors from the old life rarely brought simple problems.

"Gabriel Kane," he said. "You look like a man who's been thinking too hard."

"I need your help."

"I assumed." Ivan stood and went to a cabinet in the corner. He produced two glasses and a bottle of vodka with a label so faded it might have been blank. He poured, set one glass on the workbench between them, and leaned against the counter with his arms folded. "Tell me."

Gabriel told him. Not everything — not the Traitor, not the island, not Lyon. Just the relevant geometry: the dead-drop notification, the sedan, the designation being run by someone who wasn't him.

Ivan listened the way he did everything — with the total, unhurried attention of a man accustomed to solving problems that required patience. When Gabriel finished, Ivan drank his vodka and set the glass down.

"They're using your name to run an operation," Ivan said.

"Yes."

"And whatever that operation is, when it surfaces—"

"It leads to me. Here. Which means my cover is already compromised, whether I do anything about it or not." Gabriel picked up the glass, then set it down again. "I need to know what they're running."

Ivan was quiet for a moment. He looked at the lock mechanism on his bench. Then he said, "There's a problem."

"Several."

"A specific one." Ivan picked up a component from the bench — the lock's primary tumbler, Gabriel thought, though he'd never had Ivan's gift for mechanical intuition. "Getting into the Agency's current network means using a back-channel that's been dormant since the directorate changed. If I access it and anyone's monitoring—"

"They'll know someone's looking."

"More than that. They'll know the access point. Which puts a map directly to where I'm sitting." Ivan turned the piece in his fingers. "This quiet life I've built. It's not much. But I like it."

Gabriel looked around the shop. The workbench. The wooden birds on the counter — three of them, a wren, a heron, and something that might have been a crane. A life assembled from small, careful pleasures.

"I know," he said.

The word sat between them.

Ivan put the tumbler down and went back to the cabinet. He retrieved a second bottle — different label, higher shelf — and poured again. He handed Gabriel the better glass this time.

"You had a sedan outside," Ivan said.

"For two days."

"They're watching you but not moving. Which means they need you mobile." Ivan swirled the vodka. "They're using your designation to build a trail, and they need that trail to lead somewhere credible. A man hiding in a flat doesn't go anywhere interesting. A man who notices the sedan and runs—" He stopped. Let the implication land.

Gabriel saw it in the same moment.

The sedan isn't surveillance. It's a cattle prod.

They wanted him to run. Specifically, they needed Scholar to make contact with someone. Someone the operation required. And rather than force the issue, they were applying pressure and waiting for Gabriel's own instincts to drive him to make the move.

Which means running an operational Scholar means running me.

"They're not just using my designation," Gabriel said slowly. "They're using it to make me into an active asset without my knowledge or consent. Whatever I do next — whoever I contact, wherever I go — becomes part of their operation."

Ivan nodded. "How much of the old network are you still connected to?"

Gabriel thought about it honestly. "Enough."

"Then running you is the point." Ivan sat back down on his stool. "They don't need to brief you. They just need to panic you into moving."

Gabriel looked at the globe-studded tea cozy in his bag — he'd brought it out of habit, the way you carry the thing that grounds you — and thought about a historian who spent his career teaching people that the worst strategic decisions were made by leaders who reacted to provocations they didn't fully understand.

Don't run. Understand the board first.

"I need the operational file," he said. "And I need it without running."

Ivan looked at him for a long moment. Then he cracked a smile that was mostly resigned and slightly pleased, the way men smile when they're being dragged back into something they'd convinced themselves was finished.

"You know," he said, "the carved birds don't shoot back."

"I know."

"And the locks here are all very interesting."

"They are. I can see that."

Ivan drained his glass and stood. "Give me twenty minutes. And don't touch anything in the back room — some of it is less retired than I am."

CHAPTER 4
DIRECTIVE RESIDUE

THE BACK ROOM was a workshop within a workshop: the visible version full of tools, schematics, and half-restored mechanisms; the invisible version accessed through a panel behind the secondary safe, containing equipment that had no legitimate explanation in a coastal locksmith's inventory.

Gabriel sat at the clean terminal while Ivan worked, watching the code cascade across the screen without commenting. He'd learned years ago that watching Ivan work was like watching a surgeon: useful to observe, counterproductive to narrate.

The vodka was on the table between them. Neither of them touched it.

"There," Ivan said. "Proxy chain is holding. I've got six minutes before the monitoring protocols cycle."

He stepped back. Gabriel moved forward.

The Agency's internal file management system had changed since his time — new architecture, new naming conventions — but the underlying logic was the same. He navigated fast, muscle memory guiding his hands through a hierarchy he understood well enough to route around.

Scholar. K-412-A. Active assignments.

He found it in three minutes.

Operation RECLUSE SECONDARY.

He read it fast. Then he read it again slower, because fast hadn't covered everything and slower was making it worse.

"Ivan."

"I see it."

Gabriel hadn't said anything yet. Ivan had been reading over his shoulder.

RECLUSE SECONDARY was built on the skeleton of the mothballed X-OP RECLUSE programme — the one they'd found in the vault in Marrakesh, running through Southeast Asian fronts. Lyon's operation. Supposedly dismantled when the directorate changed.

Except it hadn't been dismantled. It had been renamed and reorganised under a new handler, and it was currently using the Scholar designation to establish credibility with a network of legacy contacts who would trust a message from K-412-A and wouldn't trust a message from anyone else.

Gabriel's name. His reputation. His history with the old network.

Being used to convince retired operatives to surface.

Not to warn them. To bring them in.

He scrolled further. The target list loaded in fragments, the file partially redacted even at the access level Ivan had opened. But enough was visible.

Eleven names. Seven already contacted using the Scholar designation. Three of those had responded. Two of those were now in custody.

At the bottom of the list, highlighted in yellow, two names with the status: *PENDING CONTACT.*

The first was a designation he didn't recognise.

The second was **W-218-F.**

The Widow.

Gabriel sat back.

They're going for Serena.

"Your designation contacted her last week," Ivan said, reading quietly. "She hasn't responded yet. Which means either she went dark, or she knows something's wrong."

"She knows something's wrong." Gabriel thought of Evelyn Marchand in a Provence vineyard, checking locks at 3 AM, living with the specific hypervigilance of a woman who'd survived things that didn't leave you. "She always knows."

"But not for how much longer." Ivan pointed at the screen. "There's a deadline in the file. If she doesn't respond to Scholar's contact within ten days—"

"They move to active recovery."

"They send a team."

Gabriel looked at the timestamp on the file. Seven days ago, the message had been sent in his name to the Widow's contact address.

Three days left.

He thought about what he would do if he received a message from his own designation and wasn't sure whether it was real. He'd ignore it. He'd wait to see if it escalated. He'd stay quiet and trust his instincts.

Three days.

"I need to shut down the Scholar contact channel," Gabriel said. "Kill the designation before they can send anything else under my name."

Ivan was already moving. "I can do that from here. But burning the channel won't stop the operation — it'll just alert them that someone found it."

"Good." Gabriel stood. "I want them to know I found it."

Ivan looked up. "Why?"

"Because right now they need me mobile. They're waiting for me to run toward someone. If I start running toward them instead —" Gabriel paused, the pattern assembling itself the way it always did, history first. *What do you do when the battle can't be won frontally? You change the terrain.*

"You force them to react to you," Ivan said.

"And reactive decisions are never the best decisions." Gabriel picked up his bag. "I'm going to Provence."

"To warn her."

"To warn her. And to give Scholar's handlers a trail that leads to a woman who is significantly more dangerous than they're expecting."

Ivan almost smiled. "And me?"

Gabriel looked at him. Looked at the workshop. The wooden birds on the counter. The comfortable, unremarkable life he'd assembled from small pleasures and patience.

"You're in the file," Gabriel said quietly. "Not on the target list — not yet. But your designation is in the system. If RECLUSE SECONDARY's handlers are auditing Scholar's contacts, they'll find the Locksmith eventually."

Ivan was still.

"I'm not telling you to run," Gabriel said. "I'm telling you what I know."

Ivan looked at the terminal screen for a moment longer. Then he closed the access window, wiped the session, and began the methodical process of shutting down the back room.

"I'll drive myself," he said. "I know a better route."

Gabriel allowed himself a small exhale.

"I'll meet you in Lyon," he said.

CHAPTER 5
THE SPARROW

BEFORE PROVENCE, there was a problem.

Seven operatives had been contacted using the Scholar designation. Three had responded. Two were in custody. The third had gone dark — no status update in the file, no location data. Either hiding or dead.

But the first seven contacts had been made through a broker. Someone who knew how to reach retired operatives who'd deliberately severed their Agency contact channels. Someone who'd sold the network's addresses to RECLUSE SECONDARY's handlers.

Gabriel knew the type. There was always a broker. The intelligence world's version of a middleman, monetising access to people who wanted to be inaccessible.

The file had named the broker in a redacted field, but Ivan had pulled the account metadata before burning the session. A routing address that traced back, through a chain of proxies, to a server in Marseille registered to a front company whose registered director was a name Gabriel recognised.

Jean-Claude Maret. Known in certain circles as *Le Moineau*.

The Sparrow.

MARSEILLE IN NOVEMBER smelled of salt water and diesel and the specific quality of a city that had survived so many different versions of itself that it had stopped worrying about the current one. Gabriel found Maret in a bar near the Vieux-Port that was dark in the middle of the day for deliberate reasons.

The Sparrow was smaller in person than his reputation suggested, which was true of most people whose reputations were built on the fact that nobody knew what they looked like. He was drinking something amber, reading a newspaper with the attention of a man who was actually watching the door, and he looked up when Gabriel sat down across from him without invitation.

"Kane," he said. No surprise in his voice.

"You knew I'd come."

"I assumed. When the Scholar channel burned, I gave it twelve hours." Maret folded his newspaper with deliberate care. "You're faster than twelve hours."

"You sold my contact list," Gabriel said.

Maret didn't deny it. "I sold a routing key. I didn't know whose list I was selling."

"You knew whose designation the buyer was using."

Maret was quiet for a moment. In Gabriel's experience, the Sparrow's silences were calculations, not hesitations. He was pricing the conversation. "What do you want?"

"The buyer's identity. Not the shell company. The handler."

"That would be expensive."

Gabriel looked at him. Not the look people used to intimidate — he'd never found that particularly effective with professionals. The look that communicated something quieter and more specific: *I know exactly how much danger you're in, I have a good idea of how much danger I represent, and I'm giving you the option to choose between them.*

Maret apparently read this clearly.

"The handler operates under a name the new directorate is

using for legacy-programme oversight," he said carefully. "Goes by Ashford. He's not Agency — he's contracted. Brought in specifically to run RECLUSE SECONDARY because he has no institutional loyalty to anyone on the old network."

"Meaning he won't hesitate."

"Meaning he won't hesitate." Maret turned his glass. "He's been careful. He used your designation precisely because it would take time for anyone to notice, and by then he'd have enough of the old network surface to justify the programme's existence to his principals."

"Who are his principals?"

"New directorate. Not Lyon's people — the ones who replaced Lyon's people. They wanted RECLUSE cleaned up quietly. Ashford's method was to surface the operatives and let the new system process them."

Gabriel thought about that word. *Process*.

"The two in custody," he said. "Are they alive?"

Maret looked at his glass. "As of last week."

"And the one who went dark?"

A pause. "I don't know."

Gabriel believed him. The Sparrow dealt in addresses and routing keys — he sold access, not outcomes. The outcomes were someone else's business, which was how people in Maret's position slept at night.

"Ashford's location," Gabriel said.

"Lyon." Maret took a sip. "He's been running the operation from a commercial office — logistics front. Third arrondissement."

Lyon. Where Ivan was heading.

Gabriel committed the address to memory and stood.

"Kane." Maret's voice stopped him. "Those two who surfaced — the ones in custody. They trusted the Scholar designation because of what it meant to them. Your name meant something."

Gabriel looked at him for a moment.

"I know," he said.

He left money on the table for Maret's drink and walked back out into the grey Marseille morning.

Seven contacts. Three responses. Two in custody.

He thought about the historian's lesson he'd been teaching for the better part of a year: that Leonidas hadn't gone to Thermopylae because he expected to win. He'd gone because he understood that the value of what you sacrifice isn't measured by the outcome of the battle. It's measured by what the sacrifice makes possible for everyone who comes after.

His name had been used to call people out of hiding.

He would use it to bring them back in.

CHAPTER 6
LYON

IVAN WAS WAITING at a café near the Presqu'île when Gabriel arrived, nursing an espresso with the expression of a man who had driven four hundred kilometres and was recalculating his retirement options.

Gabriel sat, ordered, and told him what Maret had said.

Ivan listened without interruption, which was one of the things Gabriel valued about him. The world was full of people who listened to the first half of a problem and then started solving the second half before the first half was finished. Ivan waited until the whole shape of it was on the table.

"Ashford," Ivan said.

"Contracted. No institutional loyalty. Clean hands because he's not Agency — just a man doing a job."

"And the principals want the old network surfaced and processed, and they're using your name to make the old network trust the summons." Ivan turned his cup in his hands. "What's the play?"

"We go to the office. We find the operational records — the full list, not the redacted version. We get the names of the three operatives who've already surfaced and their current locations."

"And Ashford?"

Gabriel had been thinking about this since Marseille. About the kinds of decisions that needed to be made when the math was wrong and you went in anyway.

"Ashford is a contractor doing a job. He's a problem, not a villain. If we take the records and burn the Scholar channel permanently, he has no operation. The principals lose their mechanism. The whole thing unravels because the asset they built it around just stopped cooperating."

Ivan looked at him. "You want to do this without a body."

"I want to do this in a way that leaves something useful. If we take Ashford out, the principals appoint another contractor and start over. If we take the records and make it known that the Scholar designation is dead — burned, inert, permanently inaccessible — then the old network goes back to being unreachable, and RECLUSE SECONDARY has to start from scratch."

"Which takes time."

"Which takes time."

Ivan considered this with the patience of a man who solved complex mechanisms for a living. "There's a gap," he said finally.

"Tell me."

"The records. They'll be on a system Ashford controls directly, not the Agency's main architecture. Otherwise he'd have used the main architecture and you'd never have found the dead-drop notification." Ivan set down his cup. "Which means I can't ghost the access. We have to go in."

"How much of a problem is that?"

"Depends on the physical security." Ivan's expression shifted into something that wasn't quite anticipation. "I brought some things from the back room."

ASHFORD'S LOGISTICS front occupied two floors of a building on the Rue de Sèze — the kind of address that communicated commercial solidity without drawing attention. The ground floor was genuinely a logistics company. The second floor was not.

They went in at eleven in the evening, when the ground-floor operation was dark and the building's security ran on a cycle Ivan had clocked over two hours of patient observation.

Gabriel picked the stairwell lock. Ivan managed the second-floor access panel in forty seconds.

Inside: a standard open-plan office, the lights of Lyon coming through the tall windows, everything arranged with the bland functionality of a place designed to look like exactly what it claimed to be.

Two servers in the back room. One workstation left running on a standby cycle.

"Forty minutes," Ivan said. "Maybe less."

"Take what you need."

Ivan went to work. Gabriel stood watch at the window, watching the street below. His mind, with the inexorable patience of a historian's reflex, kept returning to the same fact: two operatives in custody. People who had trusted his name.

He heard Ivan's sharp intake of breath.

"Gabriel."

The tone.

He crossed to the server room.

Ivan pointed at the screen.

RECLUSE SECONDARY had a Phase Two.

Phase One was what they already knew: surface the legacy operatives using Scholar's credibility. Phase Two was the part of the file that hadn't been visible from the Agency's system, because it wasn't filed under the Scholar designation. It was filed under the designation of each individual target.

Phase Two was the list of the people on the Agency's original Ghost Protocol roster who hadn't been accounted for.

Not eleven names. Forty-three.

And at the top, in the priority column: **W-218-F. The Widow.**

Not because she was the most dangerous. Because she was the most connected — the one whose address book, if extracted, would give RECLUSE SECONDARY every remaining contact in the old network.

They didn't just want to find Serena Marchand.

They wanted her in a room, under controlled conditions, answering questions.

Gabriel looked at the timestamp on her contact entry.

Contact initiated: seven days ago.

Response deadline: tomorrow.

"Ivan."

"I know." Ivan was already copying files to a drive. "How long to Provence?"

"Three hours. Less if you drive."

Ivan ejected the drive and closed the workstation. He looked at the servers.

"Do we burn it?"

Gabriel thought about it for exactly three seconds.

"Leave it running. If they know we found it, they'll accelerate. If they don't know yet, we have until they notice the access." He picked up his bag. "We need the head start more than we need the satisfaction."

Ivan pocketed the drive. "Very strategic."

"I've been teaching it for a year. Some of it stuck."

CHAPTER 7
VINEYARD

THE LUBERON in November was stripped back to its essential character: grey stone, bare vine rows running in long parallel lines up the hillside, the light thin and clear and carrying a cold edge that smelled of approaching rain. It was a landscape that had been producing wine longer than most civilisations had been producing history, and it wore that fact with the quiet confidence of something that had outlasted everyone's opinion of it.

Serena Marchand's vineyard was called Les Champs Perdus — the lost fields. Gabriel had always suspected she'd chosen the name herself.

He parked at the base of the hill and walked up, because arriving by car at a retired operative's home without warning was the kind of thing that ended conversations before they started.

Halfway up the path, she appeared.

She'd changed her hair. She was wearing work clothes — boots, heavy canvas jacket — and she was carrying a secateur in her right hand and nothing visible in her left, which didn't mean she wasn't armed. She watched him come up the hill with the focused stillness of someone who'd been watching the road for a week and had already modelled several versions of this arrival.

"Gabriel," she said, when he was close enough for a normal voice.

"Serena." He stopped. Let her have the distance and the positioning. "I've been using your new name. I thought you should know."

Her expression didn't change. "I know. I've been waiting to find out if you sent it."

"I didn't."

"I know that too." She looked past him at the road, then back. "How many of them are there?"

"Forty-three on the full list. Eleven contacted so far." He paused. "You're the priority."

She absorbed this the way she absorbed everything — not with reaction, but with the particular quality of attention that processes information and stores it before showing you what it's decided. He'd always found this both useful and faintly unnerving.

"Come inside," she said. "You look like you've been driving all night."

"Ivan drove."

She glanced at the car at the base of the hill. "The Locksmith's here?"

"He'll be up in a minute. He's checking the road."

The faintest softening — not a smile, but the precursor to one. "You brought him."

"I warned him. He chose to come."

She turned and walked toward the farmhouse. Gabriel followed, looking out across the vine rows — bare now, dormant, the canes tied back to the training wires with the neat care of someone who'd learned the work properly.

She built this, he thought. *She learned it from scratch, the same way she learned everything — completely, methodically, until she was indistinguishable from someone who'd been doing it her whole life.*

The Widow's civilian cover wasn't a cover anymore. It was real. Which was what made it worth protecting.

INSIDE, the farmhouse was warm. A fire. The smell of wood smoke and the dry mineral note of stored wine. Ivan arrived eight minutes later, stomping mud from his boots at the door, and Serena poured something from a bottle without a label and the three of them sat around a kitchen table that had been used for this kind of meeting before, even if the meetings had been different then.

Gabriel laid out the operational file. Everything from Lyon — RECLUSE SECONDARY, Ashford, the forty-three names, Phase Two.

Serena read it in silence. She turned pages without rushing. She didn't ask questions until she was finished.

Then she looked up.

"They want my address book."

"Yes."

"Which means they believe I'm still in contact with the others."

"They believe the Widow's network is the key to the rest of the list."

She looked at the window. Outside, the vine rows ran up into the grey November light, patient and bare, waiting for a season that was still months away.

"Are they right?" Ivan asked.

Serena was quiet for a moment. "Some of them. There are people on this list I've been quietly checking on. Not contact — just watching from a distance. Making sure." She paused. "Old habits."

Gabriel looked at her. "We have until Ashford realises we took the file. After that, the timeline changes — they'll accelerate rather than wait for the response deadline."

"How long?"

"A day. Maybe two."

She turned the last page of the file over.

"Then we have a problem," she said. "And a decision."

Gabriel waited.

"The forty-three names on this list — some of them I know. Some of them I've been watching." She looked at him steadily. "If we run, Ashford's principals put a new contractor on it and start over. If we stay, they come here and I become Phase Two's first success." She turned her wine glass slowly. "Neither of those options ends the operation."

"What does?" Ivan asked.

"The principals." She said it simply. "Ashford is the mechanism. He can be replaced. The principals are the authorisation — the new directorate faction that wants the old network cleared out before it becomes a liability." She met Gabriel's eyes. "I know who they are."

Gabriel was still.

"I've been doing what you told me to do," she said. "Going quiet, going deep, making myself hard to find. But going deep isn't the same as going blind. I've been watching." She stood and went to a dresser in the corner. From the bottom drawer, she removed a folder — not digital, paper, the kind that didn't exist in any networked system. "Fourteen months of watching."

She set it on the table.

Gabriel opened it.

Names. Dates. Financial connections. The architecture of the faction within the new directorate that had inherited Lyon's philosophy if not his methods — the belief that legacy assets were uncontrolled variables, that the old network was an institutional liability, that cleaning house was not just acceptable but necessary.

Evidence. The kind that could be verified. The kind that, placed in the right hands, would make RECLUSE SECONDARY's principals into the problem rather than the solution.

He looked up at her. "You built this."

"I've been building it since I got here." She sat back down. "I thought if things got bad enough, I'd need something to negotiate with." She paused. "I didn't expect to need it this soon."

Ivan was already leafing through the folder with the focused appreciation of a man who recognised quality work. "This is good," he said. "This is very good."

"The question," Serena said, "is what we do with it. And who we trust to deliver it."

Gabriel looked at the folder. Then at the file from Lyon. Then at the forty-three names on a list that would take an agency and a contractor and a Phase Two operation to address.

He thought about Robert in a Naples café, fourteen months ago, sliding a document across a table and saying: *This was never about revenge. Not for you.*

He thought about the deal Robert had brokered. The controlled leak. The institutional exposure that would make RECLUSE SECONDARY's principals into the story rather than the agents.

"We don't need to deliver it ourselves," he said slowly. "We need to make sure that whoever does deliver it is beyond reproach. An unimpeachable source."

"Robert," Ivan said.

"Robert. Through the oversight channel he established before Lyon fell." Gabriel looked at Serena. "Can you get this to him?"

"I can get a copy to him. But Gabriel—" She paused. "This buys time. It doesn't solve forty-three names."

"No," he agreed. "It doesn't."

The rain that had been threatening all morning arrived suddenly, rattling against the farmhouse windows, running down the glass in long irregular lines. Outside, the vine rows blurred in the grey.

Gabriel looked at them. At the bare canes tied to their wires, patient and stripped down, waiting for the spring that would make everything that had been removed this winter feel like preparation rather than loss.

"One at a time," he said. "We warn who we can reach. We give them the chance to move. We don't have the capacity to protect forty-three people — but we have the capacity to tell forty-three people that someone's coming, and let them make their own choices."

"The Retired Assassins' Club," Ivan said, with a tone that was sixty percent dry and forty percent something else.

Serena looked between them. "Is that what we are?"

Gabriel picked up his tea — it had gone cold, but he drank it anyway, the way you do when the warmth is the point rather than the temperature.

"We're the ones who got out," he said. "Which means we're the only ones who know how."

CHAPTER 8
THE RESPONSE

ASHFORD'S PEOPLE came the next morning.

Not to the vineyard — Gabriel had moved them off-site before midnight, a farmhouse three kilometres away that Serena had prepared for exactly this kind of contingency, because she prepared for everything.

From the farmhouse window, through field glasses, they watched two vehicles arrive at Les Champs Perdus at six-fifteen AM. Four operatives, professional spacing, clean kit. Ashford's methodology: contained, quiet, efficient.

They found no one.

They spent forty minutes going through the farmhouse — Gabriel imagined them finding the normal, settled evidence of a woman's life: the wine rack, the kitchen garden, the bedroom with the locks she checked at three in the morning — and then they left.

"They'll know I'm warned," Serena said. She'd watched with the same stillness she did everything, hands around a coffee cup, face neutral.

"They knew already," Gabriel said. "The file access in Lyon. They know Scholar found the operation."

"Then they know the three of us are together."

"Yes."

She nodded once, processing. "Where next?"

Gabriel looked at the list. Forty-three names. Three teams that needed warning. Twenty people he could reach through old channels and twenty-three he couldn't.

"There's a musician in Naples," he said. "Goes by Luca now. He's on the priority list — fourth behind you and two others who are already dark." He paused. "And there's an Amazon sanctuary that needs a heads up."

Ivan looked at him. "You're going to warn all of them."

"I'm going to try."

"That's a lot of driving."

"You said you were retiring from retirement anyway."

Ivan sighed. "I said no such thing."

Serena set her cup down. "I'll handle Robert. The file, the delivery, the oversight channel." She said it with the authority of someone who'd already decided this and was announcing rather than proposing. "That part is mine."

Gabriel looked at her. "When it's done—"

"I'll find you," she said. "Wherever you end up."

He believed her. It wasn't trust exactly — or not only trust. It was pattern recognition. He'd worked with her for seven years and she had never once been somewhere she hadn't meant to be.

They left at first light. Serena walked them to the car and stood in the lane as they drove down through the bare vine rows, the rain-washed morning clean and cold around her.

Gabriel watched in the mirror until the lane curved and she was gone.

Ivan drove. The road south unrolled through grey hills and pale sky, the kind of landscape that looked empty until you understood it.

"Naples," Ivan said.

"Naples."

A pause.

"The musician. What's the story?"

"He conducted black-site interrogations for six years. Now he plays jazz."

Ivan absorbed this. "Does he play it well?"

"I'm told so."

"Good." Ivan nodded, as if this resolved something. "A man should be good at the thing he chooses."

Gabriel looked out the window. Thought about a classroom in Lisbon and forty-three people who'd built their quiet lives with the same care and the same hope. Thought about the specific vulnerability of a person who'd retired from being dangerous and hadn't yet decided whether they could afford to stay that way.

He pulled out his notebook — a plain one, the kind he used for lecture notes — and wrote down the next name.

The Conductor.

Beneath it, a question he hadn't answered yet: *How do you find a man who's spent five years making himself unfindable?*

He thought about it for a while, with the slow methodical pleasure of a historian approaching a problem that had more angles than were immediately visible.

Then he wrote down the beginning of the answer.

EPILOGUE: THE LONG GAME

SIX DAYS LATER.

GABRIEL SAT in a café in Lyon — different arrondissement, different life — with a coffee he was actually drinking and his notebook open to a page covered in small, precise writing. Across from him: a chair that was temporarily empty. Ivan had gone to find croissants, because Ivan believed that difficult conversations required adequate pastry.

The news had broken two hours ago: a story in three European papers simultaneously, sourced to a single unnamed whistleblower with access to institutional finance records, detailing a covert programme within the new Agency directorate to eliminate retired field assets. Names of principals. Financial trails. Authorisation documents.

The story was accurate. Gabriel had read every word of it and found nothing exaggerated.

Serena worked fast.

His phone showed one message, sent from an address that would dissolve in twenty minutes.

Delivered. Oversight channel confirmed. Ashford's contract suspended pending investigation. Principals under internal review.

This buys months, not years. But months is enough.

The rest is yours. — S

Gabriel read it twice, then deleted it.

Ivan returned with a paper bag. He read Gabriel's expression as he sat down, processed it, and distributed the pastry.

"Done?" he said.

"Phase one."

"The principals."

"Suspended. Investigated. RECLUSE SECONDARY is on hold."

Ivan bit into his croissant. He chewed. He looked out the window at Lyon going about its morning. "And the forty-three names?"

"Thirty-one still need warning. Six I can reach this week. The rest will take longer."

"How much longer?"

Gabriel looked at his notebook. The list of names, the notes beside each one — what he knew about their cover, their location, their psychology. The specific profile of each person who'd built a new life over the wreckage of an old one.

"However long it takes," he said.

Ivan finished his croissant and poured more coffee.

"I'll drive," he said. "I drive better than you anyway."

Gabriel picked up his pen and underlined a name near the bottom of the list.

"I know," he said.

Outside, Lyon's morning moved on without them, which was the best thing a city could do.

The End

THE WIDOW

A SHORT THRILLER

CHAPTER 1
CLAIRE BERTRAND

THE ROUSSILLON SMELLED different from Provence.

Serena had noticed it the first morning — a harder edge to the air, the garrigue drier, the wind carrying something almost Spanish across the Pyrenean foothills. Provence was round and warm. The Roussillon was angular and direct, and it didn't care whether you found it beautiful or not.

She had decided she preferred it.

The domaine she was consulting for occupied thirty hectares of schist terroir south of Perpignan, owned by a widower named Mercier who had inherited it without wanting it and managed it without understanding it. Her job — *Claire Bertrand's* job, the oenologist with the clean references and the quiet manner — was to improve the blend and raise the price point. She was good at it. She'd been good at it in Provence, and before that she'd been good at far less pleasant things, and the common thread was an ability to understand systems: what each component contributed, what happened when you altered the ratios, where the instability lived.

Chemistry was chemistry.

She walked the schist rows in the early morning, the stone pale grey underfoot, retaining the night's cold and releasing it slowly into the roots. The grenache blocks needed thinning. The carignan was overproducing on the eastern slope. She noted both in the small leather book she kept in her jacket pocket and kept walking.

The cottage was a kilometre from the domaine proper — a converted outbuilding that Mercier had offered without being asked, which had suited her. Separate entrance. Separate gate. A clear sightline in every direction across flat, open ground.

She had not told Mercier she valued these features.

She walked back in the thin October light, thinking about the carignan, and found the package on her doorstep.

She stopped three metres away.

Brown paper. Twine. No postage stamp. Someone had carried it here by hand.

When? She'd been in the rows since five-thirty. The package hadn't been there at five-twenty — she'd checked the step by habit as she left. Which meant it had been left in the last four hours, by someone who knew her schedule well enough to use it as a window.

She looked at the open ground around the cottage. Nothing. The road visible for half a kilometre in both directions, empty.

Whoever left it is gone. Or watching from the domaine buildings.

She stood and looked at the package for another thirty seconds. Then she crouched and examined it without touching it — no wires, no unusual deformation, no chemical smell beyond the faint mineral note of the schist dust on the paper. She lifted it by one corner with gloved fingers and carried it inside.

On the kitchen table, she cut the twine and opened the paper with a knife.

Inside: a glass box, sealed with wax. And inside the glass, motionless against the white cotton lining —

A black widow spider.

Latrodectus mactans. She identified it reflexively, the way you identify a familiar compound. Distinctive red hourglass marking on the abdomen. Adult female, by the size. Kept alive and calm, which meant it had been transported recently and very carefully by someone who knew how.

Below it, folded twice, a white card.

I found you again, Widow. Did you miss me?

No signature. None needed.

Serena set the card down. She looked at the spider for a long moment — at the precise red marking, the stillness, the way it waited in its sealed container without apparent anxiety, without needing the situation to resolve itself quickly.

He always did like the theatrics.

She sealed the glass box, put it on the shelf above the sink, and made coffee.

CHAPTER 2
WHAT THE
SPIDER MEANS

SHE SAT at the kitchen table with her coffee and thought through it methodically, the way she thought through a new blend. Isolate each component. Understand its contribution. Then look at what the combination produced.

Component one: Le Poète found her.

She had been Claire Bertrand for four months. New identity, new region, no traceable connection to Serena Marchand or to the Provence domaine that had been raided while she was absent. She'd built the new cover carefully, from scratch, using channels she hadn't touched since her first retirement. Channels she trusted implicitly — three people, total, who had helped her construct the Bertrand identity, each knowing only their own piece of it.

Which meant either one of those three had been compromised, or Le Poète had resources she hadn't accounted for.

Le Poète — Michel Renard, born Lyon, former DGSE contractor — had crossed her path six years ago on a job that had gone sideways in the specific way jobs go sideways when your principal has been lying to you from the start. She had been sent to neutralise him. She had found him instead in a situation that fundamentally changed her read on the intelligence: not an enemy asset, not a contractor running hostile operations. A man who had been used as bait by the same people who'd sent her, left in a position designed to produce exactly the outcome they'd briefed her to deliver.

She had made a decision in thirty seconds that she'd spent six years examining from different angles.

She had left him alive. Filed the mission as a neutralisation. Told no one. Gone home and made tea and sat with the knowledge that she had just lied in an official record for a man she'd met once.

For six years that decision had lived in the closed file of things she couldn't take back. And now it was on her kitchen table in a glass box, eight legs and a red hourglass, as legible as a letter written in a language she'd spent her career learning to read.

Component two: the timing.

Gabriel had burned the Scholar designation two weeks ago. RECLUSE SECONDARY was suspended pending internal review. The directorate principals who had authorised it were under scrutiny. All of that should have reduced the active pressure on legacy operatives — the machine had been interrupted, the mechanism identified, the funding temporarily severed.

Which meant Le Poète wasn't operating through the directorate's channels. He was independent. Self-directed, privately funded, with an agenda that had existed before RECLUSE SECONDARY and would survive its suspension.

And he's in the Roussillon. Close enough to have delivered the package by hand and left before she returned from the rows.

Component three: why a spider and not a bullet?

This was the part that mattered most. A man who wanted her dead didn't send a theatrical calling card. He sent something faster and considerably less reversible. Le Poète was a professional. He knew the difference between a message and a method.

This was a message.

He wanted her to know he was here. Wanted her to react — to run, or to call someone, or to do anything that would expose her next move before she'd understood the board. It was a provocation designed to produce a predictable response from a woman trained to respond to threats.

He's underestimating how well I know his methods, she thought. *Or he's counting on me to underestimate him in return.*

She was not going to run. She was not going to call Gabriel, who was en route to Naples with Ivan and had enough weight to carry already. She was going to work backward from what she knew — the spider, the timing, the source of the Roussillon identity — and find Le Poète before he found it useful that she'd found him.

Chemistry is chemistry. You didn't fight a compound by attacking it directly. You understood its properties and its instabilities and you used both.

She thought about the channels she'd used to build the Bertrand identity. Three people, total. A documents specialist in Lyon who had produced the oenology credentials and the professional references — cautious, experienced, accustomed to not being found. A property contact in Perpignan who had arranged the consulting agreement with Mercier without connecting Bertrand to any prior identity. And a communications broker in Marseille who had built the digital footprint: the professional email history, the industry forum participation, the sparse but credible social presence that made Claire Bertrand look like someone who had existed unremarkably for a decade before arriving in the Roussillon.

Any of the three could have sold her. The question was which one, and whether the sale had been deliberate or inadvertent. Whether someone had come asking the right questions and been answered carelessly, or whether someone had been paid specifically to look and had found what they'd been paid to find.

The communications broker was the most likely point of failure. Document specialists and property contacts worked in physical materials and were consequently careful about their own exposure. People who worked in data had a tendency to believe their own systems were more opaque than they were.

She finished her coffee and opened the laptop.

CHAPTER 3
THE BROKER

HER PROVENCE COVER had been sold by a broker named Arnaud Collet, operating out of Montpellier. She'd established this quietly, three weeks after Ashford's team had raided the empty farmhouse — following the money, the methodology, the specific way that private intelligence brokers left traces in their own systems while cleaning up everyone else's.

Collet ran a network of data aggregators who compiled information on private individuals: financial records, property transactions, travel history, identity documentation. He sold it to anyone who could pay without asking why, which in her experience was the single most reliable indicator of a man who would eventually become someone else's problem.

She'd let him become hers today.

She drove to Montpellier in the afternoon, secondary roads through flat wine country, the Pic Saint-Loup visible in the distance. She parked in a public lot and walked through the lunch crowd to Collet's building — a third-floor operation wedged between a dental practice and a firm of notaires, which told her everything she needed to know about how Collet thought about himself and his work.

The outer room had a receptionist who hadn't been briefed on visitors like Serena. The inner room had Collet, who had.

He stood when she opened the door. A small man, mid-fifties, with the careful grooming of someone who needed people to take him more seriously than his appearance suggested. He'd been expecting trouble in a general sense. The specific form it had taken — a woman with very still eyes and no expression of any kind — appeared to have landed harder than anticipated.

She closed the door and sat across from him without being invited.

"You sold my previous address," she said. "And then my new one."

He started to speak. She watched his hands move toward the desk surface — reaching for a button, she thought, or a drawer with something useful in it. She shook her head once, just perceptibly.

His hands stayed where they were.

"I'm not here about the first sale," she said. "I want to understand the second. Who asked for Claire Bertrand?"

The calculation behind his eyes was almost visible — the specific arithmetic of a man deciding whether the risk of talking was smaller than the risk of not talking to the person across the desk.

"The same buyer as the first," he said.

"Describe him."

"I never meet buyers directly. Intermediary only." A pause. "The payment routing pattern — I've seen it from private intelligence contractors. Not state. Corporate shell, Luxembourg registry."

"A name."

"The intermediary used one. Once, by accident, at the end of a call." He paused. "Renard."

Renard. Le Poète's actual family name. Using it through an intermediary — either arrogance, or a deliberate signal that he wanted her to be able to trace him if she looked.

He wanted me to find him, she thought. *The spider wasn't the only map.*

"He contracted you directly," she said. "No principal above him."

"It appears so."

Self-funded. Pursuing a private agenda with his own resources. The question of where those resources came from was the next thread.

"Anything else in the file?" she asked.

Collet reached into his drawer — slowly, one hand visible throughout — and produced a thin envelope. "He paid for ongoing monitoring. Any digital movement on the Claire Bertrand identity, he wanted notification."

"Meaning he knows I came here."

"The trigger is digital movement only. Not physical." He slid the envelope across the desk. "I haven't filed this morning's movements yet."

Inside: a routing code and a partial account number. Not enough on its own. Enough to start.

"Why are you giving me this?" she asked.

He looked at his desk. "Renard paid me to find you. He didn't pay me to keep you."

A distinction without meaningful moral weight. But practically useful.

She stood. Left the envelope where it was — she didn't need the paper. "Don't file anything for two days."

He nodded quickly. She believed him because it was in his interest and men like Collet were reliable in proportion to their self-interest, which was the most honest thing she could say about them.

She walked out through the lunch crowd and back to her car, the routing code memorised and the shape of the problem slightly clearer than it had been an hour ago.

CHAPTER 4
OLEANDER AND OTHER INSTRUMENTS

LE POÈTE HAD PRIVATE FUNDING, a current location within delivery range of Perpignan, and no institutional oversight.

A man in that position didn't hide in the way institutional operatives hid — no safe houses rotated weekly, no dead drops, no surveillance detection routes. He established. He built something that looked like normal habitation, close enough to his target to monitor and far enough to feel secure.

She spent the evening mapping the routing code against what she knew of his operational preferences. He had always worked in wine country when he had a choice — she'd noted this across three operations she'd tracked him on before Marseille. Burgundy. The Rhône valley. The Languedoc. She'd assumed at the time it was aesthetics, the preference of a man who liked to eat and drink well while he worked. She reconsidered now: wine country offered cover. Seasonal workers, agricultural movement, legitimate reasons to be in cellars or outbuildings at odd hours, trucks arriving and departing without drawing comment.

The routing code traced, after two hours on clean hardware through a chain of proxy registrations, to a property rental in the Corbières. Six months. Paid in advance. Through a Belgian company that was itself registered to an address in Luxembourg that didn't exist.

A farmhouse near Lagrasse.

She knew the village. Mediaeval, walled, a small river and a ruined abbey and the particular quality of the Corbières landscape — limestone and scrub oak and an absence of pretension that she'd always found restful. Le Poète would have chosen it for the road access: two routes in, easy to monitor, easy to leave.

She packed what she needed, which was not much, and slept for four hours with the precision of someone who had learned through repetition that the quality of sleep before a difficult job mattered considerably more than its length.

She woke at three. Made tea. Thought through the approach with the unhurried care she brought to everything that mattered.

The key question was not where he was. She had that.

The key question was what he wanted. A man who intended violence didn't send a theatrical calling card three days in advance. He didn't use his own name through a broker who would eventually talk. He didn't create a trail that led, with patience and the right contacts, directly to his front door.

He wants me to come. The spider wasn't a threat. It was an invitation with an implied deadline — come before I file my location report, and we can talk. Don't come, and the report files and events proceed without me.

Fine. She would go. She would go prepared for the conversation to be something other than what it appeared, and she would leave herself the option of making a different decision than the one he expected. That was what the Widow did: she preserved options until the last possible moment, and then she exercised the one that served her best.

She finished the tea and went to the car.

CHAPTER 5
LAGRASSE

THE CORBIÈRES in the dark was limestone and scrub oak, the road cutting through it in long straight lines before twisting without warning around river gorges. Serena drove without headlights for the last three kilometres, navigating by the ambient light reflected off the pale stone — a skill she'd practised in other landscapes, on other nights, in situations where light was the thing that got you killed.

The farmhouse sat back from the road by a hundred metres, a track through plane trees leading to it. One light on in the ground floor. A dark Peugeot 5008 with rental plates parked at the side.

She parked where the plane trees gave cover, walked the last two hundred metres on the grass verge, and took twenty minutes to circle the property fully before approaching. Two entry points — front door and back. One guard at the rear of the building, she clocked him by the small orange glow of a cigarette, facing the road. He had been told to watch for vehicle headlights. He had not been told to watch for someone who came through the trees on foot and moved without sound.

She came in from the north, using the farmhouse wall itself as cover against the angle he was facing.

The cigarette was her clock. Ninety seconds from light to when he'd move or discard. She used eighty.

The back door was a standard deadbolt. She had it open in the time it took her to exhale once.

Inside: a utility room smelling of old stone and damp coats. Then a kitchen. Coffee, cigarette smoke, and underneath both something sharply chemical — she identified it in the same moment she identified the light under the inner door and the faint sound of papers moving on the other side of it.

One person. Working, not waiting.

She opened the door.

CHAPTER 6
MICHEL RENARD

THE KITCHEN WAS LARGE, a farmhouse table in the centre covered with documents and two open laptops. A man sat at the far end with his back half-turned, working by the light of a single lamp. He heard the door and turned.

Older than she remembered. The lines in his face had deepened into something more settled, the way weathered stone settles differently from new stone. His hair was shorter and greyer. But the eyes were the same — that specific quality of watchfulness that she had read in thirty seconds in a Marseille basement six years ago and which had been, in the end, the thing that decided her.

Michel Renard. Le Poète.

He looked at her for a moment with the expression of a man confirming that his model of the situation had been correct.

Then: "I thought you'd take longer."

"You left a spider on my doorstep," she said. "Not a difficult map to follow."

He gestured at the chair across from him. She didn't sit.

"The guard?" she said.

"Still at the back. I didn't brief him on the possibility of you — I didn't think he'd be useful in that context." He folded his hands on the table with a deliberateness that said he was very aware of where his hands were and what her read on them would be. "I wanted to speak with you alone."

"Which is why the spider rather than a phone call."

"A phone call gives you a choice about whether to answer." He nodded at the chair again. "Please sit. This isn't a threat."

She sat. She calculated that she could stand faster than he could close the distance if she was wrong, and she was rarely wrong about that kind of thing.

She looked at the documents on the table. Not operational files — financial paperwork. Account transfers, routing chains, the bureaucratic anatomy of money moving through institutional fictions. The kind of documents that described a funding structure to someone who knew how to read them.

"You found my locations," she said. "Both of them."

"Yes." He held her gaze. "The Provence identity first — when the directorate's operation became visible, I began looking. I needed to know where you were before they moved, and I needed to know it before you knew I was looking." A pause. "The Roussillon followed when you disappeared from Provence. I had to recalibrate."

"And then you sent a spider."

"To bring you here rather than to anyone else." His voice was even, measured. "I needed you to hear something without Gabriel Kane in the room. Because Kane will make a strategic decision about it. I needed you to make a personal one."

Serena studied him across the lamp-lit table. The last time she'd been in a room with this man, she'd been standing over him with a weapon and a set of instructions that she had chosen not to follow. He had known then what that meant — what it cost her professionally to not follow them. He had known it and said nothing and she had walked away and filed the wrong report and spent six years not thinking about whether that had been the right decision.

The thing she had not expected — that she realised now she should have — was that he had spent the same six years with the same question. That a decision made in thirty seconds could accumulate in two people simultaneously, compound differently, and produce two separate debts that had been building interest in parallel without either party's knowledge.

The spider on her doorstep was not the spider in the glass box. It was a question she'd left unanswered for six years, finally addressed.

"What did you do?" she said.

He pushed a document across the table without speaking.

She picked it up. Legacy Agency format — the kind of contract she recognised from the Lyon era, structured for deniability, layered with institutional distance. Her designation at the top.

W-218-F.

"Where did you get this?" she said.

"From the person who hired me to find you."

CHAPTER 7
THE PARALLEL TRACK

"VOSS," he said. "Not on any public record. Pre-Lyon connection to the Agency — private money, old relationships that survived the directorate change. When Ashford's operation was suspended, Voss maintained a parallel thread. Private contractors only. No Agency connection, no paper trail inside the institution."

"And you took the contract."

"He found me through my contracting history. The terms were straightforward." Renard nodded at the document. "That authorises my engagement. Below your designation, you'll find the full list of names on the parallel track."

Serena looked at the document. Twelve names below hers. Four crossed through in red — the operatives already taken before RECLUSE SECONDARY was suspended. Eight remaining, each with a designation, a last known location, and a priority ranking.

She read down the list. Sixth entry: a set of coordinates she recognised without needing to check. Amazon basin. A designation she didn't know, because the Ghost had operated in cells she hadn't crossed.

The Ghost.

"They're still running," she said.

"Ashford's suspension was institutional. This was never institutional — no ledger, no oversight, a series of private contracts paid from an account the internal review will not find because it was never on any Agency record." He met her eyes. "I was contracted to confirm your current location and report it back to Voss. The next step — a recovery team — is a separate contract to someone else, contingent on my confirmation."

"Which you haven't filed."

"Which I have not filed." He paused. "You have approximately four days before Voss will expect confirmation or begin to question whether the engagement is proceeding."

Serena set the document face-down on the table. She looked at the man across from her and thought about what six years did to a decision made in thirty seconds. How it accumulated interest. How it produced outcomes you couldn't have modelled from the original moment.

"Why?" she said.

"Because you didn't kill me in Marseille." He said it simply, without weight or drama, the way you state a fact that has been established beyond dispute. "That decision cost you professionally. I understood, eventually, what it meant that you filed the mission as complete — you protected your operational record by lying in an official document on my behalf." A pause. "You could have corrected the intelligence report without protecting me specifically. You could have flagged the faulty briefing without covering the mission. You chose the lie that kept me off the record."

"I chose it because the intelligence was wrong," she said. "You weren't what they told me you were."

"I know. But the protection was specific to me, not to the principle." He held her gaze steadily. "I've spent six years deciding what I owed you for that. Whether a debt like that could be settled at all, or whether it just accumulated interest until something like tonight."

"You don't owe me anything," she said. "It was a professional judgement."

"It was a human decision dressed in professional language." He looked at the table. "Those aren't the same thing. You know that as well as I do."

She held his gaze. The lamp between them made the silence warm and small, which felt wrong for what they were discussing.

"You spent six years deciding what you owed me," she said. "I spent six years not thinking about you at all. That's the asymmetry in your debt calculation. What you experienced as an ongoing obligation, I filed as a closed case."

"I know," he said. "That's partly why I'm here and not somewhere else." He turned his glass. "If you had thought about it, you might have made contact. Built it into the risk assessment. Instead you forgot about me, which made me safer, and the forgetting was itself a kind of generosity even if it wasn't intentional." He paused. "I'm not asking you to accept the debt. I'm telling you it existed, and that tonight is how I'm settling it. That's all."

She looked at him for a moment longer. Then she looked at the financial documents spread across the table — the money trail, the account structures, the architecture of a man who had built his safety on other people's exposure.

"You could have settled it without giving me anything useful," she said. "You could have warned me and disappeared and that would have been debt enough."

"Yes," he said simply. "But the warning alone doesn't stop the track. It just delays you." He nodded at the pocket where she'd put the contract. "That stops the track."

Outside, the guard's footsteps passed the kitchen window — unhurried, oblivious, doing exactly what he'd been told to do.

"Voss," she said. "What does he want with the Ghost?"

"Same objective as RECLUSE SECONDARY — surface the operative, bring them in. But the Ghost holds specific operational records from a buried mission that Voss has a personal connection to. He wants those records before anyone else accesses them." He paused. "The Ghost doesn't know the parallel track exists. She prepared for Ashford. She is not prepared for this."

Serena looked at the window. At the dark outside it.

A woman in the deepest jungle she could find, she thought. *Who does not know her coordinates are on a private list that a contractor has not yet filed.*

"The account Voss's payments trace to," she said.

Renard slid a second sheet across. A routing code. A Geneva property holding. A name she didn't recognise but could verify through the right channels.

"This is enough for an institutional submission," she said.

"Through the oversight channel — your contact's channel — yes. It would survive a review." He looked at the sheets between them. "I didn't retain copies. I brought you the originals."

Which meant she was holding the only copies. The contract, the parallel track's full name list, Voss's account. No parallel file in Voss's system, because that was how private contracts at this level worked — single delivery, trust the contractor, maintain plausible distance.

She folded both sheets and put them in her jacket pocket.

"What will you do?" she asked.

He leaned back, and she thought again about Marseille — about the specific quality of a man in the process of understanding that the world was not arranged the way he'd been told.

"Disappear. Properly this time — without a routing code that can be traced and without a forwarding address." A brief pause. "Without a glass box on anyone's doorstep."

"The guard."

"He knows nothing useful. I'll release him from the contract tonight." Renard looked at her steadily. "He was for appearances. In case Voss sent someone to check on the engagement's progress."

She stood and moved toward the door.

"Marchand." He used the name quietly — not Bertrand, not

Widow, not the designation. The name that was actually hers. She stopped.

"The thing I owe you," he said. "Consider it settled."

She stepped out into the Corbières night without answering. Behind her, the lamp in the kitchen went dark.

CHAPTER 8
WHAT THE WIDOW DOES

SHE DROVE BACK through the limestone country with the window open, the cold air sharp on her face, and thought about the difference between what she was and what she did.

The Widow was a codename. It referred to a specific skill set: deep knowledge of toxicology and its applications, patience as a primary tactical asset, the ability to move in social environments that required sustained performance rather than force, and the particular ruthlessness that came from understanding that slow methods were more reliable than fast ones. She had been good at all of it. She had been, for a time, the best available.

She had retired because she was tired of what it required her to be. Not the skills — skills were just chemistry and discipline and practice. What she was tired of was the reduction. The way a codename eventually became the whole of a person. The way the institution collapsed everything you were into what you could do for it.

The Widow. As though that were sufficient description of a person.

She thought about Provence. The vineyards she'd planted and tended and learned across six years. The specific satisfaction of understanding a terroir well enough to coax something genuinely good from it — not mimicking what someone else had made, but finding what that soil and that aspect and that grape variety were actually capable of and building toward it. The way that work had given her back something the other life had taken without quite naming what it was taking.

She thought about Ashford's team arriving at the empty farmhouse. The rooms she'd built a life into, swept and found uninhabited. The consulting contract she'd constructed for Claire Bertrand, the domaine she'd learned, the schist she'd walked every morning before the rest of the property woke up.

You don't grieve what you knew was temporary, she told herself. That was the rule. You built the cover knowing it was a cover. Attachment was a tactical error that she had been making repeatedly for six years and was not going to start pretending was something other than what it was.

The cottage was undisturbed when she returned. No one had been there while she was in Lagrasse. She checked by habit: the tells she'd placed in the rooms, the fine threads across the gate, the position of the glass box on the kitchen shelf. All exactly as she'd left them.

She made tea and sat at the kitchen table with both documents spread in front of her.

The contract first. Voss's name wasn't on it — this was masterclass institutional distance, a document that authorised an engagement without naming its principal anywhere in the text. But the routing code on the second sheet connected it to a Geneva property holding, and property holdings had registered owners, and registered owners were searchable if you knew where and how.

She spent an hour encoding the message to Robert's dead-drop. The Voss account, the Geneva property, the parallel track's structure and naming convention, the full list of eight remaining names. Long enough to give context. Short enough to transmit cleanly on the cipher they'd agreed in Cyprus, standing on a deck in the dark before they went over the side.

Then a second message, shorter, to Gabriel's current burner.

Ghost flagged on separate private track. Coordinates exist and are current. She needs contact now — not when you arrive. Now.

She pressed send and sat with the tea while it went cold.

Gabriel's reply came in six minutes. Three words.

Understood. Move fast.

She looked at the Amazon coordinates on the contract. She thought about fourteen hours of travel from Perpignan to the nearest reasonable access point. She thought about a woman in the jungle who had built a perimeter and set traps and prepared for RECLUSE SECONDARY and had not prepared for a private contractor with a direct coordinate and no institutional oversight slowing him down.

Ten minutes' warning, she thought. *When you know what you're doing, ten minutes is enough.*

She folded the documents and put them back in her jacket pocket and went to bed.

CHAPTER 9
THE GLASS BOX

IN THE MORNING she drove back to Lagrasse.

The farmhouse was professionally empty — the kind of clearing that said *I have done this before and I understand what a forensic search looks like.* The rental Peugeot was still at the side, which meant he'd arranged different transport in advance. She walked through the empty rooms without finding anything she'd missed the night before.

In the kitchen, on the table where the documents had been: a small glass vial. Stoppered with a cork sealed in wax. Inside, a pale yellow-green liquid she could identify by colour and viscosity without opening it.

Gelsemium sempervirens. Yellow jasmine alkaloid. Odourless, water-soluble, lethal at doses measured in micrograms, with an onset delay of forty minutes to two hours depending on the delivery mechanism. A patient weapon, which was appropriate. One of his known instruments — she'd read enough of his file to know his preferences and the logic behind them.

He had left it as a statement, not a threat.

This was what I came prepared to use, the vial said. *I chose not to.*

She held it to the kitchen window. The pale liquid moved

slowly in the morning light, viscous and almost beautiful, the way many dangerous things were almost beautiful when you understood what they were. She thought about the thirty-second decision in Marseille. About the six years of interest that decision had accumulated. About the specific form in which the debt had finally been paid.

She put the vial in her jacket pocket alongside the documents and drove back through the Corbières.

The scrub oak and limestone gave way to the flatter country of the Roussillon plain. The domaine's vine rows appeared in the distance, and she thought about the grenache blocks that needed thinning. The carignan on the eastern slope. The small leather notation book in her pocket with its careful observations about what this terroir was actually capable of, if someone took the time to understand it properly.

She thought about what it meant that she was carrying a vial of gelsemium in the same pocket as that notebook, and whether it said something meaningful about her that she didn't find the combination unusual.

The Widow's tools. The oenologist's tools. Both demanding patience, precision, the ability to read a system and understand what it would do under pressure. She had spent six years convincing herself these were separate lives. The vine rows ahead suggested otherwise — or rather, they suggested that the separation had always been something she told herself rather than something that was actually true.

Claire Bertrand would be here for another month, at the outside.

She was not going to miss it any less for knowing that in advance.

CHAPTER 10
DEPARTURE

MERCIER TOOK the news with the resigned acceptance of a man who had learned that reliable things were rarer than he'd once believed.

"Another engagement," he said. Not a question.

"Urgent. I'm sorry — I know the timing isn't ideal." She handed him the notation book. The grenache observations, the carignan analysis, the soil notes from the eastern slope. Thorough enough that any competent consultant could follow them. "The thinning on the grenache blocks should happen before the end of October. Don't let it slip past that — the production quality will suffer if it does. The carignan on the eastern slope needs a soil analysis before the next cycle; there's an iron issue in that sector that's been suppressed by the rootstock but won't stay suppressed."

He looked at the book with the expression of a man receiving instructions for something he didn't fully understand and was not sure he would be able to implement alone. "Will you return?"

"Probably not." She said it as kindly as she could, which was the most honest answer she had. "But the notes are thorough. Find someone who knows schist terroir — there are two or three consultants in Roussillon who do. Show them the book."

She left the cottage as she had found it. No trace of Claire Bertrand beyond what a legitimate oenologist would leave: boot prints in the schist, pencil marks in the domaine records, a forwarding address she would never use. She drove to Perpignan, left the car at the long-stay lot, bought a train ticket to Geneva under a third name — slower than flying and leaving fewer automated records in systems she didn't control.

At the station she bought coffee and sat where she could see both exits and thought about Voss.

She had an account number, a property holding, a name that wasn't on any public record, and a vial of gelsemium in her jacket pocket. She had a contract that only she and a disappeared contractor had ever read. She had eight names on a list that Robert was now in a position to act on through institutional channels.

The institutional channels would take days. Possibly longer.

Between now and then, Voss could issue the next contract to a different broker and adjust the approach. He had the parallel track's infrastructure and the resources to keep it running as long as the accounts were accessible. The financial freeze was not yet in place. Until it was, the parallel track was operational.

One point of remaining pressure, she thought. *Voss himself.*

She thought about what the Widow did when chemistry wasn't enough.

Then she thought about what the Widow did when patience was the right instrument and a photograph was enough.

The train pulled out of Perpignan into the pale October afternoon.

EPILOGUE: WHAT REMAINS

Geneva in the early evening was lake light and cold air and the particular silence of a city where very large amounts of money are managed with great discretion. She took a room under the third name, set the vial on the nightstand, and spent two hours in the public property registry confirming the address attached to Voss's holding.

The next morning she was outside the building at eight-fifteen, a newspaper in her hand, a coffee going cold at her elbow, watching the entrance with the patience of someone who could wait longer than the situation required.

At nine-forty, a man emerged. Mid-sixties. Conservative coat. The unhurried movement of someone who believed he had more time than events were currently allowing him.

She confirmed the face against the property records on her clean device. Took three photographs from different angles, two of which were usable. Walked away without approaching him, without any variation in her pace or bearing, without doing anything that would register as memorable in the peripheral vision of a cautious man.

She had not come to confront him. She had come to confirm he was real and findable — to give Robert's oversight contact something that could be placed in front of a committee without requiring anyone to take her word for it.

The Widow's method. Patience. Confirmation. Documentation. Let someone else make the noise.

She thought about that phrase while she walked. *Let someone else make the noise.* She had spent her operational career being the one who made the noise — the one who moved at close range, who used chemistry and timing and the specific advantage of being underestimated. The Widow's reputation had always been built on directness, on the willingness to be in the room when things happened. She had been good at it. She had been, for a time, considered among the best.

And now she was standing on a Geneva pavement taking photographs of a man's coat and walking away.

The change wasn't in what she was capable of. It was in what she wanted the outcome to look like. Renard had settled a debt by handing her documents rather than using the gelsemium. She was settling a different kind of debt — to the people on the parallel track, to the Ghost specifically, to the list of names she'd spent the last weeks trying to protect — by doing the thing that actually worked rather than the thing that felt more like the Widow she used to be.

Chemistry is chemistry. The right instrument for the situation. Sometimes that was patience and a camera and a letter to an oversight body.

She sent the photographs to Robert's channel with one line: *Voss. Geneva. Confirm this is your target.*

The reply came three hours later. Two words.

Confirmed. Moving.

She was in a café by the lake, watching the water, when Gabriel's burner sent a message.

Ghost secured. Maya is with us.

She read it twice. Thought about Amazon coordinates on a piece of paper in her jacket. A woman who had been given just enough warning to be ready for what arrived.

Good, she thought. *Warned in time is all any of us ever get.*

She typed: *Voss is identified and documented. Robert has the account and the full list. The parallel track dies when the freeze comes through.* A pause. Then: *Give me the next name.*

Four minutes.

Locksmith. Ivan already knows. Come to Berlin.

Serena folded the newspaper. Left the coffee where it was. Looked at the lake for a moment — cold and still, the Alps on the far side indifferent to everything happening along its edge.

She reached into her pocket and took out the glass box. The spider: still alive, still patient, still waiting without apparent anxiety in its sealed container. She had carried it from the Roussillon cottage without fully deciding why, and now, sitting by the Geneva lake with the case mostly resolved and Berlin waiting, she understood.

She had been carrying a question in a glass box since Marseille. For six years. And a man who owed her a debt she'd never acknowledged having had answered it, finally, by walking away from a well-paid contract and leaving a vial of gelsemium on an empty kitchen table.

Latrodectus mactans. The red hourglass, which was just a feature — a pigmentation pattern, a consequence of genetics, no more intentional than any other marking on any other creature. The spider didn't know what it signified to the people who looked at it. It didn't know it had become a symbol for a woman it had never met, standing in for a decision she'd made in thirty seconds six years ago.

Neither did I, once. She had been called the Widow for long enough that she'd stopped examining what the name meant. It had become the way the institution saw her, and then — gradually, the way these things happen — the way she'd seen herself. The woman with the poisons. The patient one. The one who waited.

She looked at the spider waiting in its glass.

That's not a self, she thought. *That's a reputation.*

The question Renard had answered — the question she'd been carrying without knowing it — wasn't whether the Marseille decision had been right. It was whether she was the person she'd been when she made it. Whether the woman who had stood over a man in a Marseille basement and chosen something other than the simplest outcome was still in there, underneath the Widow, underneath the tradecraft, underneath six years of building cover identities over the original.

The answer, apparently, was yes.

She left the glass box on the café table, on its side so the seal was down and the lid was accessible, and trusted the city of Geneva to make of that what it would.

She picked up her bag and walked toward the station without looking back.

Eight names remained. The Locksmith was one of them. Berlin was eight hours north, and Ivan Petrov had been activated once already and shown up anyway, which was the only information she needed about how that conversation would go.

The Widow had one more chapter to close before she could let the Roussillon stop feeling like a loss.

One at a time.

The End

THE GHOST

A SHORT THRILLER

CHAPTER 1
THE SANCTUARY

THE SCARLET MACAW had been at the sanctuary for eleven months before it let Maya touch it.

She hadn't rushed the process. Rushing was what made animals distrust you, and distrust in the jungle was the difference between a creature that healed and one that simply waited to die. She'd kept the macaw's pen clean and stocked, spoken to it in a low voice every morning while she made her rounds, and let it decide when the distance between them had narrowed to something it could accept.

On the morning of the eleventh month, it had stepped onto her forearm without prompting.

She'd stood very still for a long time, feeling the grip of its feet, the small weight of it, and thought: *this is what retirement is supposed to look like.*

That had been three weeks ago. The macaw — she called it Rojo, inevitably — was now in the habit of riding her shoulder during the morning rounds, which the capuchin monkey named Valdez found offensive and communicated through a series of increasingly dramatic protests from his pen.

"Eat your breakfast," Maya told him, scattering seeds through the wire. "You're not the only one here."

Valdez grabbed a seed, looked at her with reproachful eyes, and threw it back.

She moved through the morning routine the way she moved through everything — methodically, without hurry, cataloguing. Three capuchins, two spider monkeys, a juvenile tapir recovering from a snare injury, seven birds in various stages of rehabilitation, and one very opinionated scarlet macaw on her shoulder. The sanctuary had grown from a single wooden structure to a cluster of pens and cabins built over four years from salvaged timber and corrugated metal, tucked into a bend of a tributary so deep in the Amazonas state that it didn't appear on any map she hadn't made herself.

That was deliberate.

Maya Ramirez had spent four years making herself into a ghost in the most literal sense available to her: she had gone somewhere so remote that the world had simply stopped looking. Not because it had given up. Because she had made the looking too expensive.

She knew exactly when that calculation had changed.

Eleven days ago, she had received a message on the channel she'd kept open for exactly this kind of thing — a dormant frequency she'd monitored without expectation, the way you keep a fire extinguisher in a room where you've stopped cooking. The message was short and encoded in a cipher that only three people alive still used. It had decoded to eighteen words.

Parallel track running private. Your coordinates exist and are current. Get ready. Coming to you. — G

She had spent three days being angry about it.

Then she had spent eight days preparing.

Rojo shifted on her shoulder as she reached the edge of the clearing, and Maya paused, reading the bird's body language before her conscious mind caught up to why. The macaw's grip had tightened. Its head had turned fractionally toward the eastern tree line.

The birds along the eastern perimeter had gone quiet.

Maya kept walking at the same pace, finished scattering seeds for the tapir, and went back inside the main cabin. She set the seed bowl on the counter, reached beneath it without looking, and wrapped her hand around the grip of the pistol she'd moved there a week ago.

They're here.

She exhaled once. Slowly.

Good. She was ready.

CHAPTER 2
KNOWN ARRIVALS

SHE CAME out the side door and moved through the undergrowth along the northern perimeter, keeping the cabin between herself and the eastern approach. The jungle floor was soft under her boots, the light filtered green-gold through the canopy, and she moved without sound the way she'd learned to move in this specific environment — not the trained silence of an operative on a city street, but the deeper, more organic disappearance of someone who had spent four years learning to belong here.

She heard them before she saw them. Two men, moving more carefully than most would through this terrain. Not crashing. Thinking about their footfall. Experienced.

Two. She tracked their line of approach. Coming in from the northeast, following the game trail that was the most obvious path to the sanctuary from the river. She had mined the obvious path. She had not told them she'd mined it.

Stay to the left of the trail, she thought. *If you know what you're doing.*

They stayed to the left.

She stepped out of the undergrowth when they were eight metres away, pistol at her side.

"You're late," she said.

Gabriel Kane stopped. He had his hands away from his body, which she appreciated, and behind him Ivan Petrov did the same, which she appreciated more. Neither of them looked surprised to see her here rather than in the cabin. Good. She'd thought they'd know better than to expect her to wait indoors for unknown arrivals.

"I sent the message eleven days ago," Gabriel said.

"And you should have been here in nine." She looked him over. Trail dust, a cut on his forearm from a vine, the particular exhaustion that came from travelling through heat for days. Neither of them was carrying anything she couldn't see. "What happened?"

"Weather over Manaus. Then a ground delay I'd rather not explain." He looked at the cleared ground to the left of the trail. "You mined the path."

"I mined both paths. You took the right one." She holstered the pistol. "Come inside. The eastern perimeter is clean but I want you off the open ground."

Ivan said, "Hello, Maya," in the tone of a man who had learned that brevity was the appropriate register for most situations. She'd always liked that about him.

"Ivan." She glanced at his hands — locksmith's hands, she'd always thought, even before she knew what he did. Careful and precise. "How's the shop?"

"Closed temporarily," he said, following her toward the cabin. "Possibly permanently."

"I know the feeling."

CHAPTER 3
THE BRIEFING

INSIDE THE CABIN, Valdez lodged an immediate complaint about the visitors. Maya gave him a piece of mango to negotiate a cease-fire while Gabriel and Ivan spread what they'd brought on the table — physical documents, which she respected. Paper didn't ping satellites.

"Voss," Gabriel said, pointing at the top sheet.

She'd already read the name in the encoded message. "Tell me what I don't know."

He told her. The parallel track, the private account, the way Voss had structured the contracts after RECLUSE SECONDARY was suspended. The contractor assigned to the Amazon coordinates. The timeline.

When he finished, she sat for a moment and thought about it.

"The original warning said my coordinates exist and are current," she said. "How current?"

Gabriel and Ivan exchanged a look. Ivan said, "When Serena identified Voss and passed the information to Robert, she found a secondary data file in the same account structure. Satellite imagery pulled from a commercial provider. The most recent image of this area was taken four days ago."

Four days. She processed that.

"The resolution on commercial satellite over this canopy is marginal," she said carefully.

"Marginal but not useless," Ivan said. "If they know the general area and they have coordinates that are accurate to within five hundred metres, the satellite is confirmation, not location. They know where to look." He paused. "And they know the structures are occupied. Heat signature through the canopy is difficult to read but not impossible if you're looking at consistent patterns over multiple passes."

Consistent patterns. Her morning rounds. The cook fires. The animals.

"How long do I have?" she asked.

"The contractor Voss retained was a man named Briggs. He took a flight from Miami to Manaus six days ago." Gabriel looked at the table. "He knows this terrain. He's worked in the basin before, and he has a team."

"Six days from Manaus means they're already in the field." She stood and went to the window, looking out at the clearing. Rojo was on the roof of the tapir pen, preening without apparent concern. "They could arrive today."

"Or they could already be watching," Ivan said. "Setting up observation before they move."

"I know." She turned from the window. "I've been running counter-surveillance for eight days. If they're watching, they're watching from further out than I've cleared." She looked at Gabriel. "Which means they're patient. Which means Briggs is good."

"He is," Gabriel said.

"Good." She sat back down. "Then we do this properly."

CHAPTER 4
THE PREPARATION

SHE SPENT the morning showing them the perimeter.

Not the outer perimeter — they'd already navigated that — but the inner ring, which she'd built over four years for exactly this kind of situation without quite admitting to herself that she was building it for this. Pressure sensors disguised as tree roots. Trip wires at ankle height through the primary approach corridors. A series of false trails that looped back on themselves, designed to exhaust and disorient rather than kill, because she had spent four years in this jungle and some of what it had given her was a reluctance to kill things that didn't need to die.

The people who came for her would be different. That reluctance didn't extend to them.

Ivan walked the eastern approach with her while Gabriel checked sightlines from the elevated platform she'd built in the cecropia tree above the main cabin. Ivan's eyes moved over her setup with the focused attention of someone cataloguing rather than admiring.

"You anticipated flanking approaches," he said, crouching near a pressure sensor.

"I anticipated everything I could think of." She straightened. "The things I didn't think of are the things that will kill me."

He looked at her. "You've been out here four years."

"Yes."

"Alone."

"The animals aren't nothing." She paused. "And there was a period, early on, when the aloneness was the point. When disappearing completely felt necessary." She moved to the next sensor, checking the tension on the wire. "That changed. The sanctuary stopped being a cover story."

"For some of us the civilian life stays a cover story," Ivan said, without judgment.

"I know." She thought about his locksmith shop. The wooden birds. The coastal morning light. "And for some of us it becomes the actual life. I'm not sure which is more dangerous."

Ivan considered this in the way he considered most things — with the unhurried patience of a man who had learned that first thoughts were usually wrong. "I think the honest answer is that they're the same danger. You build something real and then you have something to lose."

She didn't respond, because he was right and there was nothing useful to add.

Gabriel descended from the platform and joined them on the eastern path. He had been systematic up there — she could tell from the way his eyes were still moving through the canopy, finishing the sightline calculation even while he walked.

"Three approach corridors with clean lines," he said. "The cecropia platform covers two of them. The third is the river-side approach — too much canopy cover."

"I deal with the river approach differently," she said. She led them to the edge of the tributary where it bent south — a natural channelling point where the bank was soft enough that any approach from the water would leave tracks she'd read before a person was within a hundred metres of the clearing. "The river is slower. Anyone coming from the water is committed to a route for at least twenty minutes before they reach the sanctuary. I know the sound of the water at this bend well enough that a change in the flow pattern — boat engine, significant disturbance — reads differently."

Ivan crouched at the bank. "You've been using the river itself as a sensor."

"Everything here is a sensor if you pay attention to it long enough." She looked out at the tributary. The water was moving cleanly, brown and fast, the surface showing nothing except the reflection of the canopy overhead. "The birds are the best early warning system I have. They were telling me you were coming thirty minutes before you arrived."

"The macaw," Gabriel said.

"All of them. They have patterns. When something disrupts the pattern — new presence, unfamiliar scent — the response moves through the canopy like a signal." She straightened. "Briggs will know this. If he's worked in the basin before, he'll know to move slowly enough not to trigger the birds."

"Which means he'll be close before you get the warning," Gabriel said.

"Yes." She looked back at the clearing. "Which is why the inner ring matters more than the outer one."

Gabriel was quiet for a moment, looking at the work she'd done — the layered, patient architecture of a woman who had spent four years not preparing to be found and then, in the last eleven days, reconsidering the question. "You built this in two phases," he said. It wasn't a question.

"The first three years I was building a sanctuary," she said. "The last eight days I was building a fortification."

"Is there a difference?"

She thought about it honestly. "The sanctuary was for the animals. The fortification is for me." A pause. "In the end I'm not sure I know how to build something purely for myself. Everything here has a functional purpose. The pens, the feed stores, the cleared paths — they're efficient because the animals need them to be efficient. The defences are efficient because my life needs them to be efficient."

"That sounds like the same thing," Ivan said.

"Maybe," she said. "Ask me after this is over."

Gabriel climbed down from the cecropia platform and joined them. He had a look she recognised — the look of a man who has been thinking about something he hasn't said yet.

"Operation Ghost," he said.

She waited.

"The files Serena found in Voss's account structure weren't just satellite imagery. There was a reference file — partial, encrypted, but enough for Robert to identify the programme name." He looked at her steadily. "Voss's connection to Ghost Protocol, the original one, runs through Operation Ghost. You were on that mission."

"I was."

"He was the financial architect," Gabriel said. "He designed the funding structure that ran Operation Ghost under the cover of legitimate intelligence operations. He's been exposed by Robert's submission to the oversight body — partially. The funding trail from the Ghost Protocol era, not the current parallel track."

"He's cleaning up the evidentiary chain," she said flatly. "I'm not just on the parallel track as a legacy operative. I'm on it because I was there."

"And the vault?" Ivan asked.

She had told them about the vault in the message — mentioned it in passing as a reason she couldn't simply run. She hadn't explained what was in it.

"I found it three years ago," she said. "A buried Agency cache, pre-digital era. Physical files from Operation Ghost. I stumbled on it during a survey of the tributary system and I recognised the Agency insignia on the entrance marker." She looked at the canopy.

"I didn't go in immediately. I went back six months later, with better tools, and opened it."

"What's inside?" Gabriel asked.

"Everything that the official record doesn't contain," she said. "The real mission parameters. The names of the principals who authorised it. The financial structure." She paused. "And a cross-reference to a programme called Sable. Which I couldn't identify at the time."

Ivan was very still.

"You know what Sable is," she said.

"Not exactly," he said. "But I've seen the name. In the context of Agency black-budget programmes from that era." He looked at Gabriel. "It's the funding mechanism that ran through a series of private accounts. The same accounts that ran through the Lock-smith's hands, back when the Locksmith was still working."

She understood. The vault wasn't just about Operation Ghost. The vault was the thread that connected Ghost to whatever Ivan had touched in his operational years, and that thread was now the reason Voss needed her dead before Robert's investigation got there first.

"Then we need to go to the vault," Gabriel said.

"I know." She looked at the clearing, at the animals going about their morning routines in the sunlight. "But not until we've dealt with whatever Briggs brings with him."

CHAPTER 5
BRIGGS

HE CAME AT DUSK.

She had expected dawn — the standard approach time, when defenders were at their lowest alertness and the light was just good enough to move. Briggs came at dusk, which told her he'd surveilled long enough to identify that she was most alert at dawn, and had calculated accordingly.

Good, she thought, in the narrow crease of brain that ran parallel to the action. *A competent enemy is simpler than a sloppy one.*

She had positioned Ivan in the cecropia platform forty minutes before, when the bird patterns told her something was changing at the western perimeter. Gabriel was at the secondary fallback position she'd built into the southern undergrowth, covering the approach corridor from the river.

Maya was in the clearing.

Not hiding. Standing, in the last flat light of the evening, feeding the tapir.

Briggs appeared at the eastern treeline with four men and stopped when he saw her. He was exactly what she'd expected from Gabriel's description: mid-forties, compact, the relaxed stillness of someone who had stopped needing to perform competence and simply inhabited it. He read the situation — her position in the open, her apparent unconcern — and didn't move immediately.

He's wondering if it's a trap, she thought. *It is.*

"Ramirez," he said from the treeline. He didn't raise a weapon. Neither did his team.

"Briggs," she said. She knew his name from Gabriel's briefing.

A pause. She watched him recalibrate. "You knew we were coming."

"I've known for eleven days."

His eyes moved over the clearing, assessing. She watched him register the pressure sensor near the northern pen, the tripwire at the gate of the secondary enclosure. He was good — he found two of them.

He didn't find the third.

"Then you know why we're here," he said.

"Voss wants the vault records." She didn't make it a question. "And he wants me to not be able to testify about what I know."

"More or less."

She set the feed bucket down. "I'm not going to let that happen."

He looked at her steadily. "You have two people with you. I have four."

"Yes." She met his eyes. "But you're standing in my jungle."

She raised her hand, and the eastern perimeter lit up.

CHAPTER 6
THE CLEARING

WHAT HAPPENED in the next four minutes was not chaos. Chaos was what happened when people who hadn't prepared met an unexpected situation. What happened in the clearing was the execution of a plan that had been built into the terrain over eight days of deliberate work.

The pressure sensor Briggs had missed triggered a noise charge — not lethal, but disorienting, the kind of sharp concussive crack that broke focus and reset the threat calculation. Two of his team went for cover in the wrong direction, which was the direction of the tripwire, which brought them down hard in the undergrowth.

Ivan's shot from the cecropia platform was a warning — placed six inches left of the nearest standing operative. Ivan had the range and the angle. The operative understood this and raised his hands.

Briggs himself was the problem.

He was already moving when the charge went off, moving toward Maya rather than away, the right decision for a man who understood that distance was the threat assessment's main variable. He closed twelve metres before she could fully reposition.

What followed was brief, efficient, and genuinely unpleasant. She had a reach disadvantage and she knew it and she worked around it the way she'd been taught to work around it, which was to deny him the space his reach needed by staying inside it. He hit her twice, once in the ribs and once across the shoulder, and she accepted both hits in exchange for the leverage she needed.

He went down. Hard.

She stood over him in the last of the dusk light, her ribs remonstrating and her shoulder aching, and looked at his team — two disarmed and on the ground from the tripwire, one with Ivan's rifle on him, one who had made the calculation she'd hoped he'd make and was standing with his hands up in the undergrowth.

Gabriel emerged from the southern position. He looked at her ribs with the expression of a man deciding whether to say something.

"I'm fine," she said.

"Your definition of fine has always been—"

"I'm fine."

He looked at Briggs. "What do you want to do with them?"

Briggs was conscious. He was looking at the clearing with the expression of a man updating his threat model significantly upward.

"There are six more on the tributary," he said, without being asked. "They'll come in if I don't signal within an hour."

"Six more," Ivan said from above.

Maya looked at Briggs. "Signal them," she said. "Tell them to stand down and return to the river."

"And if I don't?"

She looked at him. Not threatening. Just providing information. "Then they'll come into my perimeter, and whatever happens to them will be because of a decision you made, not because of anything they did." She paused. "Those are your people. I'm giving you the option to keep them whole."

He held her gaze for a long moment. Then he raised the radio and made the call.

She listened to the exchange. The response from the tributary confirmed the order. She watched Briggs' face while he spoke and concluded that he'd told the truth.

Good. She had enough to deal with without six more people complicating it.

"You'll stay here until we're done with what we need to do," she told him. "Then your people can collect you from the river crossing. No more engagement."

He looked at her with something that was almost professional respect. "You built this place as a fortress."

"I built it as a sanctuary," she said. "You made it a fortress."

CHAPTER 7
WHAT THE VAULT HOLDS

THEY WENT to the vault the next morning. Maya, Gabriel, Ivan. She left Briggs and his team secured at the secondary enclosure with enough water and no particular urgency about their comfort, and she moved through the tributary system the way she moved through it when she was running surveys — efficiently, reading the water and the light, the three of them quiet.

The vault entrance was a stone formation that looked, to the uninitiated eye, like an erosion feature in the riverbank — a darkened recess overhung with epiphyte roots, the stone around it worn smooth by seasonal flooding. She had spent six months looking at it before she understood it for what it was. Once you knew, the Agency insignia carved into the lintel stone was obvious.

The lock had rusted but not seized. She opened it with a tool she'd made specifically for it and led them down.

The chamber was small — roughly the size of the main cabin, with lower ceilings. Stone shelving on three walls. Metal boxes, most of them corroded, arranged by a filing system that had been meticulous when it was made and was now legible only if you understood the Agency's pre-digital archival methodology.

Gabriel moved to the boxes. Ivan moved to the shelving unit on the far wall, where a separate set of files was stored in a different format — the kind of flat-pack folders that came from a different era entirely, waterproof-sealed in something that had held better than the metal.

The smell of the vault was cold stone and old paper and a faint chemical note that she'd identified, the first time she opened it, as the specific preservative the Agency had used in its physical archive rooms in the 1980s and 1990s. She had been seven years old in 1990 and had never been in those rooms, and yet the smell was recognisable to her as institutionally specific, the way the smell of a hospital is recognisable to someone who has spent time in hospitals. It smelled like the organisation. Like its methodology. Like its willingness to store things carefully in the dark in the belief that the dark would hold.

"Here," Ivan said.

She crossed to him. The file was labelled in the Agency's operational shorthand, which she could read: *SABLE / GHOST INTER-FACE / FINANCIAL ROUTING / RESTRICTED.*

She opened it. The contents were dense — routing codes, account numbers, authorisation chains — but the structure was familiar to her from the mission documents she'd received before Operation Ghost had gone wrong. She recognised the account format. She'd seen these numbers on payment confirmations during the mission, had noted them without understanding what they represented at the time. She had been twenty-six and had believed, as you believed at twenty-six when you were new to the work, that the payment structure was the logistics team's concern and not hers.

She had been wrong about that, among other things.

"Sable was the funding channel," she said. "Ghost was the operation it funded."

"And Sable ran through a physical archive as well as a digital one," Ivan said. He was reading a separate document from the same file, his eyes moving through the numbers with the specific speed of someone for whom financial routing codes were not text but pattern. "The physical archive was secured with a proprietary key — not digital, mechanical. Designed for assets who couldn't carry electronic storage safely." He looked up. "It says the key was distributed to the Locksmith."

The Locksmith. She looked at Gabriel.

Gabriel was reading the Operation Ghost mission parameters. His expression had the particular quality of someone who finds that a thing they suspected is worse than they suspected. He read in silence for nearly two minutes, turning pages with the deliberate care of someone who wants to understand before they react.

"The mission wasn't resource mapping," he said slowly. "It was asset registration. The Agency was cataloguing human assets — informants, contacts, embedded operatives in foreign governments — under the cover of an intelligence operation. The people on those lists had no idea their identities had been recorded. The lists were then offered, through Sable, to private buyers."

"Sold," Maya said.

"Sold." He turned a page. "The buyers were governments. Private intelligence firms. Corporations with exposure in certain markets." He set the page down. "If these lists were used—"

"People would have disappeared," she said. "Informants. Embedded officials. Anyone on the list who ended up in the wrong buyer's hands."

She had known the mission was wrong. She had known it in the specific way that field operatives develop a sense for wrongness — the accumulation of small inconsistencies that don't resolve into a coherent picture, the feeling that the briefings contain elisions that matter. She had raised the concern with her team leader and been told to focus on her sector. Three months later, two of her team-mates had tried to force the issue and had died in what the official record called a navigational accident.

She had run. She had disappeared. She had let the Agency write her off as a third casualty of the same navigational accident.

She had spent four years in the jungle and thought about those two teammates frequently and about the asset lists only occasionally, because thinking about the asset lists meant thinking about the people on them and what had happened to them, and there was only so much of that she could carry while still functioning.

The vault was very quiet. The river outside moved past without commenting.

"Voss didn't fund Ghost because he was loyal to the Agency," Ivan said. "He funded it because the asset lists were a product he could sell."

"And I was there," Maya said. "I saw the data being collected. I didn't understand what I was looking at, but I was there, and I'm the last person alive who was." She looked at the file in Ivan's hands. "If the Sable key still exists—"

"It unlocks the physical archive," Ivan said. "Which means it unlocks the buyer lists. The whole chain, from Ghost to Voss to the people who paid for those names." He was very quiet for a moment. "I know where the key is," he said. "Or I know where it might be."

She waited.

"There's a woman named Elena who came to my shop," he said slowly. "Before Gabriel and I left Portugal. She brought me a key that had been her father's — an ornate, Agency-made key she said unlocked something important." He set the file down. "I looked at it briefly. I didn't recognise it then. I recognise what it is now."

Gabriel was already thinking through it, she could see the pattern-work happening behind his eyes. "You left it at the shop."

"I closed the shop when you and I left." Ivan paused. "She may have taken it back. Or she may have left it."

"We need to go to the shop," Gabriel said.

"I know." Ivan looked at the vault around them. "What do we do with this?"

CHAPTER 8
THE COST OF STAYING

MAYA STOOD at the vault entrance and thought about what to do for exactly long enough to make the right decision.

The records couldn't be moved intact — there was too much, and they had no secure means of extraction that wouldn't expose them in transit. Copies of the critical documents were possible, but partial.

"We take the Sable interface file," she said. "The financial routing and the authorisation chain. That's the link to Voss and the buyer list." She looked at Gabriel. "And we photograph the Operation Ghost parameters — as much as we can carry in memory and encrypted storage."

"And the rest?" Ivan asked.

"We burn the vault."

Gabriel looked at her. "There may be—"

"There may be things in here that are valuable to the investigation," she said. "But there are also things in here that shouldn't exist in any accessible form. Lists of human assets. Names of informants who may still be alive, who have spent years in safety because nobody knew where the records were." She looked at the shelving. "If we take those out of here, we can't control who eventually accesses them. The vault is safer than any institutional archive right now."

He thought about it. Then he nodded.

They worked for two hours. Systematic, thorough. Ivan had a memory for numbers that bordered on pathological and absorbed the financial routing codes with the focused attention of a man for whom this kind of material was legible in the way that text was legible to others. Maya photographed the mission parameters on the encrypted drive she'd kept in the sanctuary's emergency cache for this exact eventuality.

Then she set the charges she'd built into the vault entrance four years ago, when she'd found it and understood that the day would come when she'd need to close it permanently.

They stood at the tributary edge and watched the stone formation settle. No fire — the charges were concussive, designed to collapse rather than burn, to bring the riverbank down over the entrance without leaving a visible trace at the surface.

The jungle absorbed the sound the way it absorbed everything: without commentary.

"It's done," Ivan said.

"Not yet," she said.

CHAPTER 9
RELEASE

SHE WENT BACK to the sanctuary in the early afternoon.

Briggs and his team were still secured at the secondary enclosure. She had a conversation with Briggs that was brief and specific: Voss's account had been frozen pending institutional review, his contract with the parallel track was no longer operable, and the evidence that connected him to Operation Ghost was now in transit to the oversight authority. She told him this clearly and without embellishment.

He listened. He was a professional. He understood what it meant.

"The contract's gone void," he said, which was both a conclusion and a question.

"The contract's gone void," she confirmed.

She released them at the river crossing and watched them go and felt none of the things she might have expected to feel. They were a symptom, not the problem. The problem was in Geneva, and Robert and Serena were handling it.

She went back to the sanctuary and stood in the clearing for a while.

Rojo landed on her shoulder.

Maya stood with the macaw on her shoulder and looked at what she'd built — the structures she'd raised from salvaged timber, the pens she'd built by hand, the paths she'd cleared and the perimeter she'd hardened and the tributary channels she'd learned to read the way other people read roads. Four years. The longest she'd stayed anywhere since she'd gone dark.

Valdez watched her from his pen with the expression he reserved for situations he didn't understand but was monitoring carefully.

"I know," she said to him.

She had known, standing in the vault watching the charges set, that she couldn't come back to this after. Briggs' team had been stopped, but they'd been stopped by luck and preparation and the specific advantage of terrain that she'd spent years building. Voss might be financially frozen, but the parallel track had other contractors and she was still on the list and her coordinates were still on a satellite image in a data file somewhere. The sanctuary was a known location now. The only reason to stay would be if she were willing to build the fortification higher, harden it further, spend the rest of her life in a compound rather than a sanctuary.

That was not the life she had built here.

She could rebuild somewhere else. She had done it before. She knew, with the specific certainty of someone who had built a thing from nothing, that the work was possible. That the jungle was large and the right location was findable and the structures could be raised again with different hands and the same patience.

She also knew, with an equal and opposite certainty, that she was not going to do it. Not immediately. Not until the list was down to zero and the parallel track was dead and Voss was past the point of being able to issue another contract.

One more mission, she thought. *One more, and then you come back to this.*

She opened Valdez's pen first.

He came out, looked at her, looked at the open gate, looked at her again with the reproachful intensity of a small creature who was aware something significant was happening and wasn't certain he'd been adequately consulted about it. He sat on the gatepost for four minutes, which she counted. Then he dropped to the ground, picked up a seed from the feed scatter on the clearing floor, and moved toward the tree line with the unhurried authority of a creature whose circumstances had just improved considerably.

She watched him go until the canopy took him.

The spider monkeys next. They left as a group, which she'd expected — they'd been brought in together, a family unit found after a habitat clearance, and they'd maintained the social structure throughout their rehabilitation. The eldest paused at the tree line and looked back at her, and she wasn't going to attribute human intention to the look but she noted it anyway and stood still until they were gone.

The other capuchins. The birds she released through the aviary roof, opening the hatch and standing back, and most of them went immediately, the way birds do when a door opens, without reflection, into the available sky. Two of the smaller ones perched on the hatch edge for a moment and she thought they'd come back to her hand but they didn't, and that was right.

The tapir she walked to the tributary. It had been here the longest — found in November of her second year, dragging a snare wire that had cut deep into its rear left leg. She had treated the wound over six weeks, and the leg had healed imperfectly, with a slight favouring on the rough ground that would smooth out over time. She walked it to the bank, watched it test the water with its nose, and watched it enter and cross to the far side and climb the bank on the other side without looking back.

She had read somewhere that tapirs were largely solitary and had good spatial memory, that they would establish a home range and return to it reliably, and she thought about that now — about a creature navigating by remembered landmarks, building a map of the world through repetition and return. She had done the same thing for four years, mapping this tributary system until she knew it well enough to navigate in the dark, and the thought of navigating it in someone else's dark — without the specific landmarks she'd built, without the morning rounds and the feed routines and the particular quality of the light at six AM over the cecropia platform — was a grief that she recognised as disproportionate and didn't argue with.

Rojo left her shoulder when she opened the aviary. Lifted off, circled once low over the clearing in the specific way that looked like a decision and probably wasn't, and was gone into the canopy. She watched the red shape until it was only a flicker and then nothing.

Gabriel and Ivan were behind her. She didn't hear them but she knew they were there the way you know the presence of something that has learned to be quiet in the same terrain you have.

"Ready?" Gabriel asked.

She looked at the empty pens. The cleared paths. The morning light moving across structures she'd built by hand for reasons she hadn't fully understood until they were finished.

"Yes," she said.

EPILOGUE: THE NEXT NAME

THEY TOOK the tributary system north to the river and the river to the airstrip, which took most of the day. Maya carried the encrypted drive and the Sable interface file and nothing else from the sanctuary. She had kept a pack ready for four years at the emergency cache, and she took that, and she did not go back to the main cabin.

On the river, with the canopy moving overhead and the water brown and fast around the boat, Ivan laid the Sable interface documents on the floor of the boat and read through them again with the concentrated attention of a man solving a problem he already understood the shape of. He had a way of reading financial documents that reminded Maya of the way she read the jungle — not word by word, but by recognising pattern deviations, things that shouldn't be where they were.

"The routing structure is sophisticated," he said eventually. "Whoever designed Sable understood that the most vulnerable point of any black-budget operation is the funding chain. Auditable records, traceable transactions — they expose everything eventually." He looked at the water. "So they built Sable to run backward. Funds moved from untraceable private accounts into the operation, rather than from Agency accounts outward. On paper, Ghost looked self-funded. Consultant fees. Equipment procurement. The kind of line items that an auditor would pass over."

"Which made Voss invisible," Gabriel said.

"More than invisible. If you looked at the accounts from the outside, you'd conclude Ghost was an operation funded by private intelligence contractors who had a legitimate interest in the output." Ivan folded the documents carefully. "The Agency got the intelligence. Voss got the asset lists. The contractors got plausible cover. Everyone's interests aligned."

"Except the assets," Maya said.

"Except the assets," Ivan agreed.

"Elena," he said finally. "The woman with the key."

"Her father was on the Ghost mission," Gabriel said. "Not as an operative — as a contractor. He was the physical custodian of the Sable archive. The key she brought to me was the archive key." He paused. "I left it in the shop."

"Do you think she went back for it?"

"I don't know." His voice was careful. "But if she didn't, and the shop has been accessed since we left—"

"The key is what Voss is actually after," Gabriel said from the bow. "Not Maya specifically. Not us. The buyer lists in the Sable archive." He turned. "Maya was the last witness who could testify to the connection between Ghost and Sable. But the archive itself is the real exposure — if someone presents those buyer lists to the oversight body, Voss isn't just financially implicated. He's criminally implicated. The people who bought those lists are implicated." He paused. "We're not talking about an institutional review anymore. We're talking about something that ends careers and possibly ends people's freedom."

"Which is why he kept the parallel track running after RECLUSE SECONDARY was suspended," Maya said. "Not to clean up legacy operatives. To get to the archive before Robert's investigation did."

The river moved. The canopy overhead shifted and showed sky in pieces — brief blue rectangles that closed and opened as the trees moved in the afternoon wind. Maya watched them and thought about the vault, sealed now under several tonnes of riverbank, its contents reduced to what she carried on the encrypted drive and what Ivan had absorbed through those careful eyes of his.

It's enough, she thought. *It has to be.*

She thought about the tapir crossing the tributary. About Valdez sitting on the gatepost for four minutes before deciding the situation had improved. About Rojo circling once over the clearing, that red flash against the green, before the canopy took him.

One more mission.

Gabriel's phone buzzed. He read the message and held it up.

Serena's number. Two words.

Berlin. Now.

He looked at Ivan. "Serena's at the shop."

Ivan exhaled, something in his posture releasing that had been held since they'd left the vault. "She found it first."

"Or she found the problem first," Gabriel said. "Which is the same thing with Serena."

Maya looked out at the river. The Amazon moving past them, unhurried, carrying everything downstream without comment or judgment, the same water that had been moving through this basin before any of them existed and would be moving through it long after they were done with their particular complications.

Thirty names remaining, she thought. *Thirty people in their quiet lives, built over old lives, not yet knowing.*

"Then we go to Berlin," she said.

The End

THE LOCKSMITH

A SHORT THRILLER

CHAPTER 1
LIFE ON THE COAST

THE LOCK HAD BEEN BROUGHT in by a retired schoolteacher named Senhora Faria who had inherited it from her mother, who had inherited it from her mother, who had apparently acquired it in circumstances that Senhora Faria described as *"best left vague."*

Ivan Petrov had been working on it for three mornings.

It was a Bramah-style lock from the late nineteenth century — not a reproduction, the genuine article, with a barrel mechanism of a complexity that the original designer had advertised, correctly, as unpickable. The advertisement had been made in 1784 and had stood unchallenged for sixty-seven years before an American locksmith named Alfred Hobbs had opened one at the Great Exhibition in London in 1851, which Ivan thought said something useful about the nature of apparently impenetrable systems.

He'd been spending a lot of time thinking about apparently impenetrable systems lately.

He turned the lock in his hands, feeling for the particular relationship between the notched key and the barrel's internals — not forcing it, just listening, the way you listened to an engine or a person when you wanted to understand what was actually happening rather than what appeared to be happening. Through the window of the shop, the Portuguese morning moved at its usual unhurried pace. Fishing boats in the harbour. The smell of bread from the café two streets up. A dog sleeping in the specific patch of sunlight it had claimed as personal property for the three years Ivan had lived here.

He was aware of all of it and paying attention to none of it, which was how he operated most mornings: technically present, actually somewhere else.

The wooden birds were on the counter. He'd carved seven of them over the past month — a wren, a heron, something that might have been a crane if you were generous, and four smaller birds whose species he hadn't decided yet. He left them there for customers to take if they wanted one. Most of them did. Senhora Faria had taken two on her last visit and reported that her grand-children had named them and given them an elaborate social life. Ivan had found this more satisfying than he had words for.

This was the life he'd built. Locks and birds and the morning light off the harbour and a regularity so complete that he'd started to forget what its opposite felt like.

You're in the system, he thought. *Gabriel said so. Ivan Petrov, Lock-smith designation, on a list that a private contractor named Voss is working through from a Geneva address.*

The knowledge had arrived with Gabriel two weeks ago, delivered in the calm, factual manner of a man who had moved past the stage of finding such things surprising. They had drunk Ivan's better vodka and mapped the situation and agreed on a plan, and then Gabriel had left for Naples — because Luca was the priority before Ivan, the Conductor higher on Voss's list — and Ivan had returned to his shop and his antique locks and his carved wooden birds and his apparently quiet life.

Which was not, in any meaningful sense, quiet anymore.

He set the Bramah lock down and went to make tea, and on the way to the kettle he checked, by habit and without appearing to, the three tells he kept at the shop's entry points: the thread at door-height across the back corridor, the chalk mark on the window latch, the position of the bird he'd left on the step outside that morning. All undisturbed. The shop was still his.

He made tea and sat with it and thought about Voss, and about the buyer lists that Maya had found in the Amazon vault and that Serena was apparently now using as the basis of a submission to an oversight body in Geneva, and about whether the submission would be enough. The financial freeze was procedural — it inter-rupted Voss's operations but didn't end them. The buyer lists were something different. The buyer lists were the kind of evidence that ended careers and, in some cases, ended freedom, and the people on them were not the kind of people who accepted that outcome quietly.

He was thinking about this with the specific concentration of a man trying not to think about it when the bell above the shop door rang.

Ivan looked up.

CHAPTER 2
THE KEY

SHE WAS YOUNG — mid-twenties at most — with dark eyes that were doing the specific work of trying to look calmer than she was. She carried a worn leather satchel slung over one shoulder and stood in the doorway for a moment before deciding to come in, which told him she'd been outside longer than the bell suggested, making a decision.

"Are you Mr. Petrov?" she asked, in accented Portuguese that said she'd learned it recently and under pressure.

"Just Ivan," he said. "What can I do for you?"

She came to the counter and opened the satchel and set something on the glass. A key. He looked at it before touching it: ornate, Agency-made, the alloy specific enough that he placed it before he consciously decided to. The etching on the teeth was a pattern he had seen once before, in a different country, on a different piece of hardware, a very long time ago.

Sable.

He kept his expression neutral. "Where did you get this?"

"My father left it to me." She held his gaze with the direct determination of someone who had practised this conversation. "He died eight months ago. I found it in his things. His name was Aldo Ferretti — I don't know if that means anything to you."

It didn't, but the key did. He picked it up. Turned it. Felt the weight and the specific resistance of the mechanism — not a standard key, a partial key, designed to work in combination with a second element. The symbols on the teeth were a cipher sequence. He had seen the same sequence, or a version of it, in a set of documents he'd been asked to courier during a job in Warsaw, years ago, for a programme he'd never been fully briefed on.

Sable. The word had appeared in Maya's message last week. *Cross-reference to a programme called Sable. Which I couldn't identify at the time.*

"Your father," Ivan said carefully. "What do you know about his work history?"

"Not much," she said. "He told me he was a technical contractor for European government clients. I thought it was data systems. I found the key and some documents after he died — encrypted, mostly. But one page had a name on it." She paused. "Petrov."

Ivan looked at her. "He sent you to me."

"He wrote a letter. To be opened if anything happened to him." Her jaw tightened slightly. "Something happened to him."

"What?"

"He said it was a heart attack." She met his eyes. "He was fifty-one and had run a marathon the year before."

Ivan set the key down on the counter between them, equidistant. "Your name?"

"Elena Ferretti."

"Elena." He looked at the key. Then at her. "Sit down. I'll make tea."

CHAPTER 3
WHAT THE KEY OPENS

HE'D BEEN ABOUT to explain when the shop door opened again and two men walked in who were not there for locksmithing services.

Ivan clocked them in the first second: dark jackets, weight distributed for concealed carry, the specific quality of alertness that said *professional* and *briefed*. One of them had a scar along his left cheekbone that Ivan didn't recognise but filed. They moved with the unhurried confidence of people who believed the situation was already resolved.

"We're looking for an object," the scarred one said. "A key. We were told it was brought here."

Ivan kept his hands visible on the counter. "People bring keys here constantly. I'm a locksmith."

"This one specifically." The man's eyes moved to Elena, then back. "Hand it over and we'll leave you both in peace."

They were watching the shop. Which meant they'd followed Elena, or they'd known she was coming, which meant they had access to something in Ferretti's documents or communications. Either way, the timing was five minutes too late — they'd let her get inside, which meant they wanted to hear the conversation, not interrupt it. They'd lost patience when no key appeared on the counter.

The scarred man's eyes moved to the counter surface, and Ivan saw him clock the key where it sat between the Bramah lock and the tea things. A mistake — Ivan should have pocketed it when Elena put it down. He filed that as a lesson and didn't show it on his face.

Ivan picked up the Bramah lock he'd been working on and set it beside the tea things with the specific unhurried calm of a man doing nothing threatening. His right hand was now six inches from a set of pick tools that were not, strictly speaking, weapons, but that a man with thirty years of experience handling precision instruments could use in ways the manufacturer had not intended.

"Wrong place," he said pleasantly.

The scarred man's jaw tightened. His partner took a step toward the door, blocking it.

Ivan had built this shop with three exits and had used none of them in three years for anything other than inventory delivery.

He used one now.

He was around the counter before the scarred man could recalibrate, moving Elena toward the back corridor with his left hand and using his right to hook the stool he kept behind the counter into the path between them and the front door. Not a weapon — a delay. A one-second disruption in the geometry.

One second was enough.

They went through the back, into the alley, and Ivan kept them moving through the town's rear streets — the paths he'd walked every morning for three years specifically so that he could navigate them without thinking. Left at the textile warehouse. Right through the covered market passage. Down the steps to the lower harbour road where the tourist traffic was thick enough to absorb two fast-moving people without comment.

Elena kept pace. She was in good shape, which he noted professionally. She didn't ask questions until they'd covered four blocks and ducked into the archway of an old textile warehouse, and then what she asked was: "Who were those men?"

"People who also know what your key opens," Ivan said. "Which means we need to move faster than I'd planned."

He looked back the way they'd come. No immediate pursuit visible, but that meant nothing — professionals didn't pursue visibly.

"Your father's letter," he said. "Did it say anything about coming to me directly? Or did it give you other instructions first?"

"It said come to you first. It said you would know what the key meant." She held his gaze. "Do you?"

"Yes," he said. "Come with me."

CHAPTER 4
THE ARCHIVE

THEY WENT to the secondary space Ivan kept for exactly this eventuality — a storage unit in the harbour district, rented under a name that didn't exist, which held a change of clothes, two burner phones, enough cash for two weeks, and a small metal case containing equipment that had no legitimate explanation in a locksmith's inventory.

He'd told himself for three years that he kept it there because a man with his history was prudent to maintain contingencies. He'd been mostly honest with himself about what it actually was.

He opened the case while Elena sat on the upturned crate he kept for the purpose, and he looked at the key properly for the first time without a counter between him and it.

The teeth pattern was three-sequence: a standard mechanical profile, then an etched cipher layer, then a third element that required a physical companion piece to complete the circuit. He'd seen this construction before — not this specific key, but this architecture. It was Agency-made, custom-fabricated, and designed for a physical archive rather than a digital one. The archive required the key *and* a sequential code that would have been memorised rather than written, because writing it was the kind of security failure the programme's designers had been paid specifically to prevent.

"The Sable archive," he said, half to himself.

Elena looked at him. "You know what it is."

"I know what the key is for." He set it down. "The Sable programme ran a physical archive — documents that couldn't be digitised because the people involved couldn't risk the exposure of a networked system. The archive was secured with a proprietary key distributed to the programme's physical custodian." He looked at her. "Your father was that custodian."

She absorbed this with the particular stillness of someone processing information that confirms a worst-case suspicion. "What's in the archive?"

"Buyer lists," Ivan said. "The people who paid for intelligence from Operation Ghost — an Agency operation that harvested human assets and sold their identities to private buyers." He held her gaze. "Your father held the key that could prove who those buyers were and trace the financial chain back to the man who organised the sales."

"Voss," she said.

He looked at her.

"The letter," she said. "My father's letter said that if I needed to use the key, I should find Petrov and say the name Voss. That Petrov would understand what it meant."

He understood what it meant all right. Ferretti had known, apparently, that the Locksmith designation was connected to the operation in a way Ivan himself hadn't fully grasped until Maya's message last week. He had couriered Sable documents in Warsaw without knowing what they were. He'd handled part of the puzzle without ever seeing the whole.

His phone — the burner, not the shop line — buzzed.

He checked it.

Serena. Two words.

Outside. Now.

CHAPTER 5
THE TEAM

SHE LOOKED like a woman who had been travelling for eighteen hours and was annoyed about it, which was exactly what she was.

"You could have opened the door," Ivan said.

"I wanted to confirm the space was clean first." Serena stepped inside, looked at Elena with the specific quality of assessment that said *assigning a role*, and looked at Ivan. "Gabriel's four hours out. He's bringing the Ghost."

"Maya."

"Maya." She sat on the second crate and looked at the key on the table. "Is that it?"

"That's it."

She leaned forward, studying it without touching. "The archive. Do you know where it is?"

"Not yet." He looked at Elena. "Your father's documents. The encrypted ones — did any of them contain coordinates? Location references? A city?"

Elena opened the satchel and produced a folded paper. "I've been carrying this since I left Rome. The letter said the documents would be readable to the person who had the key." She set the paper on the table. "I couldn't read them. But I thought maybe—"

Ivan picked up the paper. It was a printed page, heavily encrypted — a standard Agency block cipher layered over what appeared to be a property document. He looked at the cipher structure. The key in his hand had a secondary function: the teeth pattern, read as a sequence rather than a mechanism, decoded a specific substitution cipher. He'd worked with this architecture once, years ago, in a context he was only now connecting to this moment.

He worked through it in ten minutes. The property document underneath described a storage facility in Berlin — a converted government building in the Schöneberg district, with an access code and a room designation.

"Berlin," Serena said.

"Berlin." Ivan looked at her. "Which is where you were."

"Which is where I was." She looked at the paper. "Voss has an address in Geneva but his operation runs through Berlin. The account I identified for Robert traces to a property management company registered there." She paused. "The submission I filed through the oversight channel — the financial freeze — that's institutional. Slow. It buys time but it doesn't close the case."

"The buyer lists close the case," Ivan said.

"If we can get them in front of the right people, yes." She met his eyes. "Not just Voss. The people who paid for those lists. Governments. Firms. People who are currently untouchable because the financial chain doesn't go all the way back to them."

"It goes back to the archive," Ivan said.

"Which requires the key." She looked at Elena. "Which means your father put this in the right hands after all."

Elena looked at the paper, at the key, at the two people around her who were moving through this conversation with the specific ease of people for whom this kind of situation was the register of ordinary. "What do I do?" she asked.

"You stay close," Ivan said. "And you don't touch anything in the archive without permission."

She looked at him steadily. "My father died for whatever is in that archive."

"I know," he said. "That's exactly why."

CHAPTER 6
BERLIN

GABRIEL ARRIVED with Maya four hours later, at the secondary harbour space, and the five of them occupied the crates and the floor in the particular compressed way of people who have learned to be functional in small rooms.

Maya assessed the space in two seconds and positioned herself near the door, which Ivan noted and appreciated. She had the specific environmental awareness of someone who had spent years reading terrain as primary information. She looked different from how he'd imagined her based on Gabriel's descriptions — smaller, more still, with eyes that moved like a sensor sweep rather than a glance.

Gabriel looked at the key, the decoded document, and Ivan with the expression of a man completing a calculation he'd started in the Amazon. "The archive was in the Sable documentation," he said. "Maya found the reference in the vault. We knew the key .existed and that it had been distributed to the custodian. We didn't know the custodian had a daughter."

"My father knew you'd come eventually," Elena said. "Or someone like you. That's why he left the letter."

Gabriel looked at her with the particular quality of attention he gave things that mattered. "Ferretti. Your father's name."

"Yes."

"He was careful." It wasn't quite a compliment but it was close.

Serena spread the decoded document on the crate that was serving as a table and oriented the group around it. "Berlin. Schöneberg district. The facility is listed under a municipal records management company — legitimate cover, probably converted in the early 2000s when the Agency was consolidating its physical archives." She tapped the address. "I know this street. I was in Berlin for three days before I sent the message."

"What were you doing in Berlin?" Maya asked.

"Following the Voss account trail. After I identified him in Geneva and filed the submission through Robert's channel, I knew the financial freeze was temporary. Procedural holds get lifted when the right people make the right calls. I needed to understand the operational structure — what Voss was running beyond the parallel track, where the Berlin connection went." She looked at the document. "I didn't find the archive specifically. But I found the property management company. I was two steps away."

Ivan looked at her. "You didn't tell Gabriel."

"I told Gabriel there was a Berlin connection and to come." She held his gaze without particular apology. "I didn't know about the key yet. I didn't know about Elena. I was working with incomplete information, same as everyone else."

"Welcome to the club," Maya said, which was the driest thing Ivan had heard anyone say in recent memory, and he'd spent two weeks at sea in his own company.

They took the overnight train to Berlin — not together, not in the same compartment, with the specific distributed configuration that made five people into five separate journeys. Ivan sat with his tools case in the overhead rack and the key in his inside pocket and thought about lock architecture, which was what he always did when he was anxious.

Every lock was a conversation between the designer and the future person who would try to open it. The designer's side of the conversation was: *I know things you don't, and I've built those things into this mechanism, and you will have to understand all of them before you can proceed.* The opener's side was: *Tell me everything you know. I am listening.*

He had been listening to locks for thirty years. The Sable archive's designer had been very good — physical, mechanical, non-networked, multi-factor. But good wasn't the same as perfect, and perfect wasn't the same as permanently sealed.

I am listening, Ivan thought. *Tell me everything.*

CHAPTER 7
THE ARCHIVE

THE BUILDING in Schöneberg was exactly what the property document had described: a converted government storage facility, unremarkable, brick-faced, occupying the ground floor of a building otherwise used for municipal document retention. Ivan walked past it twice before entering.

The storage section was accessed through a side entrance with a standard electronic keypad — Voss's people had upgraded the outer security at some point in the last decade, which was the kind of thing that happened when a programme's custodian died and new principals decided they needed tighter control. The electronic lock was not the lock Ivan was here to open, but it was in his way.

He opened it in forty seconds.

Inside: corridors, document shelves, the smell of old paper and the specific cold of a room kept at controlled temperature for preservation purposes. The room designation from Ferretti's document was B-14. They found it at the end of the lower corridor — a door with no electronic access, which was right. The inner lock was the original.

Ivan crouched in front of it.

The mechanism was a dual-factor physical lock: the ornate key in his pocket plus a sequential tumbler code that corresponded to the cipher sequence on the key's teeth. He'd worked out the sequence on the train — it read from the teeth pattern as a series of six positions, each corresponding to a tumbler setting. The designer had been elegant about it. The key itself contained its own companion code, for the person who knew how to read it.

He took a moment before inserting it.

This was the thing most people didn't understand about locks: the moment before opening was as important as the opening itself. You didn't rush it. You built a complete mental model of the mechanism — the relationship between the key's profile and the barrel's pins, the sequence of movements that would resolve the system into its open state — and you committed to that model before you touched anything. Because a wrong move in a complex mechanism didn't just fail to open it. It could set it back, or in the worst designs, trigger a failsafe that permanently sealed it.

He had seen failsafe designs before. He was fairly certain this one didn't have one — Ferretti had needed the archive to be accessible, not just securable — but fairly certain was different from certain, and the difference mattered.

He built the model. Confirmed it against what he knew of the cipher sequence. Breathed out once.

He inserted the key. Aligned the first position. Felt the tumbler settle.

Second position. Third.

The mechanism was smooth for a mechanism this old — someone had maintained it. Ferretti, probably, on his visits to confirm the archive was intact. The small, careful gestures of a custodian who understood that what he was keeping needed to remain openable by the right person when the time came.

Fourth position. Fifth.

The sixth tumbler was the interesting one — a false position designed to reset the mechanism if you applied pressure before the fifth had fully seated. A trap for the impatient or the uninformed.

Ivan held the pressure off the sixth until he felt the specific give that said *five is ready,* and then he moved to six, and the lock opened with the particular satisfaction of a conversation correctly concluded.

He pulled the door.

"Well done," Serena said quietly, and he thought she probably meant it as straightforwardly as it sounded.

CHAPTER 8
WHAT FERRETTI KEPT

THE ROOM WAS SMALL — four metres by three, shelving on three walls, a table in the centre. Files in sealed plastic sleeves. A secondary case bolted to the back wall, combination-locked, which Ivan opened in under a minute because it was a commercial safe and commercial safes were a different conversation entirely.

Inside the case: three drives, labelled in Ferretti's handwriting with dates and programme codes. And underneath them, a letter.

Not encrypted. Just sealed. His name on the front.

Petrov —

If you're reading this, the key reached you and you opened the archive. My name is Aldo Ferretti and I was the Sable programme's physical custodian from 1998 to 2011. I kept these files because I understood, eventually, that the people who commissioned the programme intended to use the buyer lists again. Not as historical intelligence. As active leverage.

The drives contain everything: asset lists from Operation Ghost, buyer identity records, financial routing, authorisation chains. Every transaction. Every name.

I couldn't go to the oversight bodies myself — I had Elena. I couldn't risk it. But I kept the archive intact, and I kept the key, because I believed that eventually someone would come who could use it properly.

The man who wants this archive is named Voss. He is not the only one. The buyer lists implicate people who are currently in positions of institutional authority. Some of them are in the intelligence community. Some are in government. They will not stop pursuing this archive until it is either in their hands or publicly exposed.

Expose it. That's all I'm asking.

— Ferretti

Ivan read it twice. Then he passed it to Gabriel without speaking.

Gabriel read it. Passed it to Serena. She read it and passed it to Maya, who read it standing up with the same focused attention she gave everything, and then set it carefully on the table.

Elena hadn't moved. She was watching the letter move around the room the way you watch something that contains your father.

"Can I read it?" she asked.

Ivan looked at Gabriel, who nodded. He picked up the letter and brought it to her.

She read it in silence. He watched her face — the specific progress of a person encountering a document that confirms what they'd half-suspected and still doesn't prepare you for the confirmation. The part where Ferretti wrote *I had Elena* — he saw her stop there, briefly, before continuing.

When she finished, she folded it along its original creases. She held it for a moment. Then she set it on the table beside the drives.

"He was protecting me," she said.

"Yes," Ivan said.

"By not telling me." She looked at the drives. "By keeping all of this, keeping the key, keeping the archive intact — for twenty-five years — but not telling me, because telling me would have made me a target."

"That was his calculation," Ivan said. "Whether it was the right one—"

"It was the right one." She said it simply, without apparent ambiguity. "I was seventeen when he received the key. I was twenty when he must have understood what the programme was actually doing. I was twenty-five when I finished my degree." She looked at Ivan. "There was never a right time to tell a child that her father was protecting evidence that powerful people would kill to suppress." A pause. "Until there was a right time, and the right time was when he was gone and couldn't be used against anymore."

Ivan thought about Ferretti sitting alone with these drives for twenty-five years. Building the encoded letter. Keeping the key. Living a normal life over a hidden one, and doing it not for himself but for a daughter who would never know the shape of what was underneath until he was past needing her protection.

"He was very careful," Ivan said, which he had said before and meant more fully now.

Maya was at the shelving, reading file labels with the specific focus of someone who had spent years in a jungle learning to read what was actually there rather than what she'd expected to find. "The asset lists," she said quietly. "The names from Operation Ghost." She looked at Ivan. "These are the people whose identities were sold."

"Some of them may still be alive," Ivan said.

"Some of them." She set the file down carefully. "Some of them won't be."

The room was quiet for a moment. The controlled temperature hum of the archive. The faint sound of the street above.

Elena was looking at the drives. "My father held this for twenty-five years," she said. "Not for justice — he didn't know if justice was possible. He held it because he thought it should exist. That the truth should exist somewhere, even if no one ever found it." She looked up. "He was right about that."

Gabriel passed the letter back. "We take the drives. We leave the physical files — some of the asset identities should stay sealed. Copying them widens the exposure."

"Agreed," Serena said. She was already at the table with a clean device, copying the drive contents under controlled conditions.

"Robert's oversight channel. Same method as the Voss account submission. Coordinated release — financial records first, buyer identities second, authorisation chain third. Each element implicates the next."

"How long?" Gabriel asked.

"To copy? Twenty minutes. To submit? I can have it filed within the hour." She looked up. "The financial freeze on Voss's account was a procedural hold. What we're submitting now is criminal evidence. Different tier of response."

"He'll know it's coming," Ivan said. "If he has any contacts in the oversight body — and a man like Voss always has contacts — he'll have a window."

"A short one," Serena said. "But yes."

CHAPTER 9
VOSS MOVES

THE WINDOW WAS TWENTY-THREE MINUTES.

Ivan knew this because he was watching the street outside the archive building while Serena copied the drives, and at the twenty-three minute mark a vehicle he hadn't seen before turned into the street and parked at the far end in the specific position of something that intended to cover the exit.

"We have company," he said.

Gabriel was at the window in two steps. He studied the vehicle for a moment. "Private contractor. Not Agency — wrong vehicle spec, too clean for surveillance, too present for a tail." He looked at Ivan. "Voss moved faster than we expected."

"He had someone watching the electronic lock," Ivan said. "When I opened it, he had a notification."

"How far is Serena?"

"Twelve minutes," Serena said, without looking up. She had clearly been following the conversation.

The vehicle at the end of the street wasn't moving. Two men inside, visible in profile. Waiting for something — a signal, a second team, a confirmation from somewhere else.

Maya was at the back of the room, looking at the secondary exit

Ivan had identified on the way in — a fire door at the corridor's end, alarmed but not locked, opening to an internal courtyard. "Courtyard leads to a parallel street," she said. "If they've covered the front, they may not have covered the parallel. It's a longer walk to the vehicle."

"They'll cover it when they hear the alarm," Ivan said.

"Yes." She looked at him. "Which is why we want the alarm to go off after we've been in the parallel street for sixty seconds, not at the same time."

He understood. "I'll delay it."

He went to the fire door and opened the panel beside it — an older model, the kind of alarm integration that had been installed when the building was converted and never upgraded because nobody expected anyone to care about a municipal document storage facility's secondary egress. He found the delay circuit in forty seconds and gave it an extra ninety seconds of lag.

"That's the best I can do," he said.

"Good enough," Maya said.

"Serena," Gabriel said.

"Done." She ejected the drive, pocketed it, and closed the archive room door behind them. "Filed. Both submissions — the Voss account and the buyer lists. The oversight body has every-thing. It's out of our hands now."

Ivan looked at the room one last time. The shelves. Ferretti's careful files. The case with the combination lock that had opened in under a minute.

Tell me everything you know, he thought. *I was listening.*

He pulled the door shut.

CHAPTER 10
THE PARALLEL STREET

THEY WENT through the fire door in single file and across the courtyard at the pace of people with somewhere specific to be who were not running, because running created attention and attention was the thing they couldn't afford in the next ninety seconds.

The parallel street was a residential road, quiet mid-morning, a woman with a pram and two men talking outside a café and no one who looked like Voss's contractors.

Sixty seconds.

They walked north, unhurried, until the fire alarm reached its delayed trigger and a quiet electronic tone began behind them — immediately answered, Ivan knew, by the two men in the vehicle at the front of the archive building.

By then they were three blocks away.

"Car," Gabriel said. He made a call on his burner in less than thirty seconds, and seven minutes later a vehicle arrived — a contact Serena had established during her time in Berlin, a former operative who now ran a private transport company and occasionally did work that didn't appear in the company's accounts.

They drove south, out of Schöneberg, through the city. Nobody spoke for the first ten minutes.

Then Maya said, from the back: "The buyer lists are going to name people who are currently protected."

"Yes," Gabriel said.

"The oversight body will sit on some of it. Protect the institutional relationships."

"Probably."

"Robert's contact," Serena said. "He's outside the institutional structure. The submission goes to him first. He decides what surfaces publicly and what goes through formal channels." She looked at Gabriel. "That was always the plan. The oversight body gets the financial evidence. Robert's contact gets the names."

"And Voss?" Elena asked. She had been quiet since the archive. Processing, Ivan thought — not shutting down, organising.

"Voss loses the archive and the financial chain in the same seventy-two-hour window," Ivan said. "The freeze becomes a criminal investigation. The buyer lists make him a witness they need rather than a principal they're protecting. He has no leverage left." He paused. "He may run. He may cooperate to reduce his exposure. Either way, the parallel track is finished."

Elena turned the key over in her hands. She had taken it from the archive when Ivan returned it to her — it belonged to her, he'd said, which was the simplest accurate statement he could make about a thing that had cost her father twenty years of quiet fear. "My father held this for twenty years," she said.

"Thirteen," Ivan said. "He received it in 1998. He died eight months ago."

"Twenty-five years," she said.

"Twenty-five years." He looked at the key. "He built a good archive. Clean, organised, intact." He paused. "He was careful in the way that only people who understand exactly what they're protecting are careful."

Elena looked at him. "Did you know people like him? In your work?"

"Some." He thought about the Warsaw courier job. The documents he'd handled without knowing what they were. The specific, deliberate blindness of an operational structure designed to protect its assets from understanding the whole. "More than I knew at the time."

She was quiet for a moment. Then: "Thank you for opening it."

"That's what locksmiths do," he said.

It was not the most profound thing he had ever said. But she smiled at it, briefly, and that seemed like the right ending for that particular exchange.

EPILOGUE: THE NEXT NAME

They split at the central station — the natural dispersal of a team whose work in this location was finished.

Elena had a decision to make about what came next, and Ivan had given her the best information he had and left the decision to her, which was the right thing to do when the decision belonged to someone else. She had her father's key, her father's letter, and a clearer picture of her father's life than she'd had a week ago. What she did with that picture was hers. She had asked Ivan, before they separated, whether the archive would have protected anyone on the asset lists who was still alive, and he had told her honestly: some, probably, and that would depend on how quickly the submission moved through the oversight process and whether the right people acted on it before the wrong people suppressed it. She had nodded and looked at the key in her hand and said, "Then I want to be there when it surfaces. Not hidden somewhere. Present."

He had not tried to talk her out of that. A woman whose father had spent twenty-five years hidden, making something that could only matter in the open — he understood why she needed to see it reach the light.

Serena left first, with the copy of the drives and a destination she didn't share, which Ivan respected. She would be filing, verifying, managing the submission process through Robert's channel with the same methodical competence she brought to everything. He'd worked with her twice before, years ago, and had always thought that the Widow designation undersold her — the patience it implied was real, but what drove it was less about waiting and more about understanding systems well enough to know exactly when to move.

She had moved, this time, precisely when it mattered.

Maya stayed in the station café with Gabriel and Ivan for twenty minutes over coffee that none of them were really drinking.

"The parallel track is broken," Gabriel said. "Not dead. But broken. Voss's account is frozen, the buyer list evidence is filed, the financial chain is in Robert's hands. The contractors who were running under the track's authorisation have no valid contracts." He turned his coffee cup. "The list still has names on it."

"How many?" Ivan asked.

"After Elena — twenty-nine."

Twenty-nine people in their quiet lives. Ivan thought about his shop. The antique locks. Senhora Faria's Bramah mechanism, which he had been about three hours from solving when Elena walked in. The dog that owned a particular patch of sunlight on the pavement. The carved birds on the counter, which would still be there — he'd locked up but not cleared out, because he hadn't decided yet whether the shop was finished or just temporarily closed.

He thought about the Bramah lock, which Hobbs had opened in 1851 after the manufacturer had spent sixty-seven years believing it was permanently sealed. The manufacturer had been wrong, but the lock had been very good. The distinction mattered.

"I'm going back to the shop," he said.

Gabriel looked at him.

"It's compromised," Ivan said. "I know that. I'll go back, close it properly, and leave." He paused. "But I want to finish the Bramah lock first."

Maya looked at him with an expression that suggested she understood exactly what he meant and was not going to say so, which he appreciated. She had the quality of a person who understood that some things didn't need to be explained and were not improved by explanation.

"The Conductor," Gabriel said. "Luca. He's the last name on the priority list."

"I know." Ivan had heard the name from Gabriel at the start of all this, and again in the Amazon, and had been turning it over since. Luca was a jazz musician in Naples who had spent five years building a life as far from his operational past as Ivan could imagine, which was a significant distance. "Have you warned him?"

"I warned him at the end of Scholar. He knows the situation. He hasn't moved yet." Gabriel's expression had the quality of a man who had learned not to predict what Luca would or wouldn't do. "Which is either wisdom or stubbornness."

"With musicians," Ivan said, "it's usually both."

He thought about Luca's situation — the jazz club, the Naples life, the specific stubbornness of a man who had decided that his civilian identity was the version of himself he intended to keep. He understood it. He understood it more than he'd understood it three weeks ago, before a schoolteacher's daughter had walked into his shop with a key that had been waiting for him specifically.

Ferretti had spent twenty-five years as a man with a secret underneath his ordinary life, and that secret had not diminished his ordinary life — it had given it a particular weight, a meaning beyond itself, the specific dignity of a person who is carrying something important quietly. Ivan had spent three years as a locksmith. A genuine locksmith, in the end. The cover had become the thing.

He was not entirely sure that *cover* was still the right word.

He finished his coffee. Stood. Checked the exit by habit and found it clean.

"I'll drive," Maya said. She was looking at a train board with the expression of a woman calculating routes, which Ivan suspected was not entirely what she was calculating.

"You always say that," Gabriel said.

"I'm always right about it."

Ivan pocketed the empty burner and picked up his tools case and thought about the Bramah lock, about Senhora Faria, about the particular pleasure of a mechanism that had kept its secrets for a hundred and forty years and was now, finally, three hours from telling them.

Every lock is a conversation, he thought. *And every conversation ends eventually.*

He walked toward the exit and didn't look back.

The End.

THE CONDUCTOR

A SHORT THRILLER

CHAPTER 1
THE OPENING ACT

THE MAROON SUIT had cost him three weeks' wages and he wore it like armour.

Luca stepped to the edge of the stage, adjusting his cuffs, and looked out at the crowd through the low light of the club. A hundred faces, none of them paying attention to the specific thing he was doing, all of them paying attention to the general impression he was making. This was the deal with jazz: the audience thought they were listening to music. What they were actually doing was being conducted — their attention directed, their emotional temperature managed, their sense of time dissolved and rebuilt at his discretion.

He had understood this before he understood music. He had always understood rooms.

The club was called Cinque Note, which meant Five Notes, which was either a reference to the pentatonic scale or to the five founding members of the partnership that had owned the building before Luca bought them out two years ago. He had kept the name because it was already on the sign and because he had spent enough of his life erasing things without needing to erase a perfectly serviceable name for a jazz club.

The piano was a Fazioli. He had bought it before he had enough money for it, which was the right order of priorities.

He raised his hand.

The band came in. Upright bass first, the pulse of it settling into the room's bones before the piano followed, and then the saxophone finding the pocket and the space between the bass and the piano and Luca's own voice, which wasn't a voice but a presence, the specific quality of standing very still at the centre of organised chaos and knowing that everything is proceeding exactly as planned.

This was the parallel to the work he had done before. The Conductor — his operational designation — had referred to his ability to run multiple assets simultaneously from a central position, coordinating information flows and human behaviour without ever being the person who appeared to be in charge. It had been extraordinarily useful in black-site interrogation programmes, in political influence operations, in the specific discipline of making a room produce the outcome you needed without anyone in the room understanding they were being managed.

He had retired because he had decided that the thing he was good at deserved better applications.

He wasn't entirely sure the jazz club was better. But it was real, and it was his, and every night when the music was right he felt something that he was fairly confident was a version of the thing other people meant when they talked about peace.

This is what retirement looks like, he thought, for the hundredth time, and for the hundredth time he was not entirely convinced by it.

He played the room for forty minutes. He knew it was forty minutes because he had designed it to feel like twenty — that specific quality of an audience that doesn't want to stop. When he signalled the final chord and the applause came, it came with the particular warmth that meant he'd got the temperature exactly right.

He bowed. Straightened. Scanned the room with the automatic surveillance sweep he'd never been able to stop doing, even after five years of pretending it was just stage fright management.

Third table from the bar. A man in a dark jacket with his hat pulled low, who had been there when Luca arrived and had not yet ordered a second drink, which meant he wasn't there for the music.

Matteo Ferri raised his glass in a slow, deliberate salute.

Luca kept his face in the post-performance configuration — warm, open, slightly distracted — and stepped off the stage.

CHAPTER 2
MATTEO

THE BAR WAS CROWDED ENOUGH that a conversation could be had quietly. Luca leaned against it, ordered water he didn't need, and let Matteo come to him, because a man who wanted something was better assessed when he was doing the approaching.

Matteo moved with the specific economy of a person who had spent years being paid by the day and had learned that visible effort was expensive. He was three years older than Luca and looked five years younger, which Luca had always found vaguely resentful.

"Didn't think Naples was your scene," Luca said.

"It isn't." Matteo set his glass down. "But you are."

Behind them, the band was running through a quiet interlude. Someone at the back of the room laughed at something — a generous laugh, full-throated, the laugh of a person who was exactly where they wanted to be. Luca filed it and kept his attention on Matteo.

"The storm," Luca said. "You mentioned a storm."

"Still coming." Matteo's eyes moved over the room with the same automatic sweep Luca used, which told him they'd been trained in compatible methodologies. "There's an auction in three days. Private villa, invitation only, the kind of guest list that doesn't exist in writing." He paused. "The Maestro will be there."

The name landed the way names like that always landed — not with shock, because Luca had been waiting for it since Gabriel's message arrived six weeks ago, but with the specific weight of a thing you've been carrying becoming visible.

"What's being auctioned?" Luca asked.

"An encryption matrix." Matteo's voice was flat. "The original operational cipher from a programme called Sable."

Luca looked at his water glass. "And you're telling me this because—"

"Because I was on the list," Matteo said. "The parallel track. I've been running ever since I got the notification. I've been watching the Maestro's people move through Naples for two weeks, and I know what they're here for, and I know I can't stop them alone." He met Luca's eyes. "I know you got the same warning I did. The Scholar sent it."

Gabriel. Who had warned Luca six weeks ago, in a message that decoded to seventeen words: *Parallel track still running. You're priority five. Someone is coming for the Sable cipher. Get ready.*

Luca had spent six weeks getting ready.

"The auction," he said. "Who's the Maestro?"

Matteo looked at him steadily. "That's what you need to find out."

From backstage, a crash. The sound of glass, and a voice calling out — Marco, the saxophonist, unmistakably Marco's voice, with the particular edge of someone who was hurt and scared at the same time.

Luca was moving before the echo faded.

CHAPTER 3
THE BRIEFING

THE CORRIDOR behind the stage was narrow and dark and smelled of old wood and instrument cases. Marco was on the floor with a shard of glass in his leg and a look on his face that Luca had seen on other people in other corridors and had hoped never to see on someone who played saxophone in his jazz club.

"I slipped," Marco said, and then, when Luca was crouching beside him: "I didn't slip. Someone was here. I heard—"

"I know," Luca said. He helped Marco up, handed him to the bandmate who'd appeared in the doorway, and turned to look at the window at the corridor's end.

Closed when he'd done his walkthrough three hours ago. Open now.

A soft knock on the wall behind him.

"Don't," said a familiar voice, "reach for anything dramatic."

Gabriel Kane was leaning against the corner with his hands visible and the expression of a man who had learned that entrances into enclosed spaces should be preceded by some kind of signal. He had the look of someone who had been travelling for two days on not enough sleep, which in Gabriel's case meant he looked slightly more intense than usual.

"You're late," Luca said.

"Six weeks late," Gabriel agreed. "The message I sent—"

"I got it." Luca stepped past him back into the corridor. "The cipher. The Maestro. Three days." He looked at Gabriel. "I've been working."

Gabriel's expression shifted slightly — the specific recalibration of a man who had come prepared to explain a situation and finds it's already been explained. "How much do you know?"

"Matteo Ferri is in the club. He's been on the parallel track, he has an auction location, and he knows the Maestro will be there." Luca kept his voice level. "I don't know who the Maestro is. I have a theory, which I've been unable to confirm without resources I don't have in a jazz club in Naples."

"Tell me the theory."

"The directorate principals," Luca said. "The ones Robert's submission named. The financial freeze on Voss's account, the buyer lists from the Sable archive — all of that hits the institutional principals. But Voss wasn't operational. He was money and structure. Someone was running the operational side."

Gabriel looked at him for a moment. "The Maestro is the Sable programme's operations director. He ran the actual mission — coordinated the asset extraction, managed the contractors, ensured the product reached the buyers." He paused. "His name is Carlo Orsini. He spent five years listed as a casualty of an unrelated operation."

"He faked his death."

"He faked his death." Gabriel straightened. "And now he's trying to recover the one piece of the Sable operation that wasn't destroyed — the original cipher matrix. Without it, the buyer lists can be denied as fabrications. With it, they're verifiable, and every transaction in the archive traces back to authorised signatures."

"His signatures," Luca said.

"Among others."

From the club beyond the curtain, the band had resumed — a gentle, quiet number that the audience would accept as the interval between sets. Luca could hear it the way he always heard music when he wasn't performing it: analytically, as a series of decisions, each one about what to give the room and what to withhold.

"I have a contact who can get us into the auction," Luca said. "But we're going to need more than just entry."

Gabriel's phone showed a message. He turned the screen toward Luca.

En route. Eight hours. — S

Serena. And behind her, if the sequence held, Ivan. And Maya.

Luca allowed himself, briefly, the specific satisfaction of a room that was coming together.

"Then we have eight hours to plan," he said. "Let's use them."

CHAPTER 4
THE PERFORMANCE

THE VILLA OCCUPIED a headland south of Naples with the specific confidence of a building that had never needed to justify its existence. Stone walls, iron gates, a guest list that arrived by private courier rather than email, and security that had been arranged by people who understood that visible deterrence was for amateurs.

They had been visible amateurs. The visible deterrents did not deter them.

Getting in had required three days of planning and one conversation with Matteo that Luca had found illuminating in ways beyond the immediate operational requirement. Matteo knew people who knew people, which was the whole of what Matteo had always been — not an operative in the directional sense but a node, a person through whom information flowed and connections were made and obligations were kept or called in. He had given them the invitation under Edoardo Costa's name without apparent difficulty, which told Luca that Matteo's value to the network they were dismantling had been precisely this: not loyalty, but access.

The three days of planning had covered the villa's layout, the security rotation, the guest demographics, the auction's structure, and two contingency protocols for scenarios they hoped not to use.

Gabriel ran it with the methodical precision he brought to every-thing — not exciting, but the kind of thoroughness that prevented the specific category of problem that killed people. They had worked from the basement of a rented apartment three streets from the club, at a table covered in satellite imagery and route maps, and Luca had found that he had not forgotten how to do this work. He had simply not been doing it.

The planning was where the Conductor designation actually applied. Not in the field — in the field he was a capable operative, no more, no less. In the planning room he was something different: the person who could hold the whole composition in his head simultaneously and understand how each part related to every other part, where the vulnerabilities were and where the strengths were and what the piece needed to resolve correctly. Gabriel was better in the field. Maya was better in terrain. Ivan was better with mechanisms. Serena was better at chemistry and patience.

Luca was better at the room. At reading what a situation required and building the conditions in which the team could deliver it.

This is what the codename meant, he thought, walking through the main gate. *Not the interrogations. This.*

He walked through the main gate in a tailored mask and a jacket that had cost more than his first month's rent in Naples and belonged to a man named Edoardo Costa, who had been an arms dealer in the 2000s and was understood in certain circles to have spent the last fifteen years in a comfortable and unexplained retire-ment in Argentina. Luca had used Edoardo once before, years ago, in a different context. The invitation had been arranged by Matteo, who had his uses.

Behind him, at the appropriate social distance, Serena moved in silver filigree and the specific ease of a woman who had been in more dangerous rooms than this. Ivan was already inside, having arrived forty minutes earlier as part of the catering arrangement that Maya had organised through a contact whose name Luca didn't know and had agreed not to ask. Gabriel was on external surveillance, positioned where he could see the villa's three exits and the service road.

"Earpiece check," Gabriel said quietly.

"Clear," Luca said, without moving his lips.

"The Maestro's people confirmed present. Eight security personnel, four guest-facing, four back-of-house. The auction starts in forty minutes." A pause. "Orsini hasn't been visually confirmed yet."

"He'll be here," Luca said. "He wouldn't send someone else for this."

The ballroom was everything it needed to be — chandeliers, champagne, masked figures who moved with the practiced confidence of people who existed in spaces where no one asked pointed questions. Luca took a glass and moved through the room with the unhurried attention of a man doing several things at once: presenting as a guest, mapping the exits, reading the security rotation, and listening for the specific frequency of heightened alertness that preceded an operation going wrong.

He found the frequency thirty seconds in.

The security personnel were too present. Not obviously — they hadn't broken the guest-to-security ratio that would suggest imminent action. But they were watching Luca specifically. Not the way security watched everyone: the way security watched someone who had been identified.

They know I'm here. Not Edoardo Costa. Luca Moretti, the Conductor.

He kept moving. Took a sip of the champagne without drinking it. Found Serena three minutes later near the east wall and let his eyes do the work.

She gave the smallest possible nod. *I see it too.*

CHAPTER 5
THE AUCTION

THE AUCTIONEER HAD a voice designed for rooms like this — warm, authoritative, the sound of money being formalised. The first three items were what you would expect from a black-market auction dressed in legitimate clothes: intelligence fragments, political leverage, the kind of thing that cost a government ten years of careful tradecraft and sold here for what a mid-tier consultant made in a quarter.

Luca stood near the back of the auction room and watched the bidders and thought about tempo.

Every room had a tempo. The art of conducting was understanding that tempo before it became visible — reading it in the way people stood, the speed at which they turned their heads, the rhythm of their breathing. In a jazz club it was the audience: you could feel when they were ahead of you and when they were behind, when they needed to be given something and when they needed to have something withheld. The auction room was running at a specific tempo, and that tempo was wrong. Too controlled. The guests were masked and anonymous, but they were moving with a collective suppression that said *we are waiting for something specific and we already know what it is.*

This wasn't an audience. This was a cast.

"Balcony, north side," Maya said through the earpiece. "Silver mask. Two interlocking M's."

Luca counted to three — long enough to seem casual, short enough to be useful — and let his gaze drift north and up.

The man in the silver mask was standing with the quality of absolute stillness that said *I have already decided how this ends.* The interlocking M's caught the chandelier light and scattered it in two small arcs. He was flanked by two people who were clearly security and one person who might have been an assistant or might have been a third security operative — the ambiguity was deliberate, designed to make an accurate threat assessment difficult.

Luca spent four seconds on it. He concluded: third security operative. The pen in the possible-assistant's jacket pocket was too thick for a pen.

"Confirmed," he said quietly.

He spent the next ten minutes making himself useful as scenery. Accepting a refill he didn't drink. Speaking briefly to a man in a peacock mask about the weather in Monaco, which the man appeared to believe was a coded reference to something and Luca allowed him to continue believing. Moving through the room in the specific way that said *I am comfortable and unhurried and exactly where I choose to be.*

The security rotation confirmed what he'd read on entry: four personnel tracking him, one of whom was the third balcony operative who had come down to the floor during the second auction item. Orsini knew Edoardo Costa was a fiction. He'd known it before Luca walked in the door.

The question was whether he'd known long enough to prepare a response, or whether he'd identified the cover in the last few hours and was still building his reaction.

The auctioneer's voice shifted register — the particular elevation that preceded a significant lot. "Ladies and gentlemen. Our final item this evening represents a unique opportunity. The encryption matrix for the Sable programme — the original operational cipher, authenticated and complete."

The room held its breath.

A case was brought forward. Glass-fronted, locked. Inside, a drive and a physical codebook sealed in an evidence sleeve — the kind that Agency archivists used to certify provenance. The drive was a copy, Luca knew from Serena's pre-operation intelligence — the original had been in the Berlin archive. But the codebook was real, the encryption keys physical rather than digital, and without it the drive's contents were unreadable and therefore unverifiable and therefore deniable.

Orsini had spent two years building toward this moment. Getting the drive out of the archive before Ivan and Serena could seal it off. Getting the codebook from a source that had taken years of patient relationship-building. Bringing both to a room full of buyers who would pay anything for the ability to suppress a truth.

"The matrix cannot be broken without the original key," the auctioneer continued. "Possession of this item provides the means to verify — or suppress — any intelligence derived from the Sable programme's operations."

A gloved hand rose from the balcony.

Luca raised his own hand.

The room turned. He felt the shift the way he felt the shift in a room when the first note landed differently than expected — a collective reassessment, a sudden presence of possibility that hadn't been there a moment before. The security personnel were recalculating. The guests were recalculating. And up on the balcony, behind the silver mask, Orsini was recalculating.

"The conductor's baton," Gabriel said through the earpiece, his voice carrying the dry quality of a man who'd spent years watching Luca operate. "You have thirty seconds before his security repositions."

"I need twenty," Luca said.

The auctioneer, admirably composed, said: "Do we have a counter bid?"

Luca smiled — the specific smile he used when he wanted a room to understand that he was the most confident person in it. "We do."

CHAPTER 6
CONTROLLED CHAOS

THE LIGHTS DIED at the precise moment Luca had calculated they would.

Not because he'd cut them himself — because Orsini had, and Luca had read the room's tempo correctly and known it was coming. When you understood a conductor's methodology, you could anticipate the downbeat.

The difference was that Luca was already moving.

He stepped left before the emergency lights came up, putting the auctioneer's podium between himself and the position he'd been standing in. A professional marksman with night optics would have fired at where he'd been. In the two seconds it took for the room to adjust, Luca covered four metres and reached the service door he'd identified during the entry walkthrough.

"East exit, now," he said. "Ivan, the case."

Ivan's voice was already moving: "I have eyes on the case."

The auction room was dissolving into the specific chaos of a crowd that had trained itself to expect eventualities and was now encountering one it hadn't anticipated. Serena was a shadow through the confusion, moving toward the point where Luca was heading, her bearing unchanged.

"Orsini is off the balcony," Maya said. "He's going east."

East. The same direction as the case. Which meant Orsini's exit plan and Luca's intercept vector were converging on the same corridor.

This was either a problem or an opportunity. Luca decided it was an opportunity.

He came through the service door into a corridor lit by a single emergency strip — low, red, the colour of a stage just before a performance begins. At the far end, the Maestro moved with the unhurried precision of a man who believed he had already won.

Luca had seen that quality before. It was the tempo of a performer who had confused control with certainty.

"Orsini," he said.

The silver mask turned.

The man behind it was in his sixties — lean, sharp-boned, with eyes that had the specific quality of someone who had spent decades reading situations and was accustomed to finding them legible. He was holding the glass case. The drive and the codebook were intact.

"The Conductor," Orsini said. "You're a long way from your piano."

"So are you," Luca said. "From whatever you are when you're not wearing that."

Orsini looked at him with the particular patience of a man who has decided not to rush. "You understand that taking this changes nothing. The buyer lists are in the oversight body's hands, yes. But without verification — without the cipher matrix — they're allegations. Circumstantial. Deniable." He paused. "I've been doing this for forty years, Luca. I know exactly how far evidence has to reach before it becomes fact."

"I know," Luca said. "That's why I'm not here for the case."

Orsini's eyes shifted fractionally.

"The case is Ivan's problem," Luca said. "I'm here for you."

CHAPTER 7
TEMPO

WHAT FOLLOWED WAS NOT, strictly speaking, a fight. A fight required two people both trying to hurt each other. What happened in the corridor was more like a negotiation conducted under time pressure, with physical arguments replacing verbal ones.

Orsini was good. Luca had expected good — a man who had faked his own death and run an off-books intelligence operation for a decade without surfacing was a man with capabilities. He moved with the economy of someone who had trained consistently rather than extensively, which was more dangerous than the reverse. There was no wasted motion. Every action was the minimum required, which was the signature of a practitioner rather than an enthusiast.

Luca was better, specifically in one way: he had spent five years doing nothing that looked like operational work, and he had spent all five of those years maintaining the readiness to do operational work, which was the specific discipline of a person who understood that the civilian life was real and the operational readiness was also real and neither cancelled the other. The pianist's hands. The conductor's stillness. The capacity to stand in the centre of a room and let everything that needed to happen flow through him without getting in the way of it.

He took two hits. He gave four. The fourth one was conclusive.

He stood over Orsini in the red-lit corridor and felt his ribs register a complaint about the second hit and decided to deal with it later.

Orsini was conscious. He looked up at Luca with the expression of a man running calculations that were not resolving in his favour.

"The matrix is already gone," Luca said, because there was no point in Orsini continuing to calculate around that particular variable.

"Ivan," Orsini said. Not a question.

"Ivan." Luca looked at the man on the floor. "You knew we'd be here."

"I knew you'd try." Orsini shifted, testing whether he could sit up, and found he could. He did so with the careful dignity of a person refusing to have the conversation horizontal. "I didn't know you'd be this prepared. Your team has improved."

"We've had practice," Luca said.

Orsini looked at him with the particular patience of a man who had decided not to rush. "You understand that taking this changes nothing. The buyer lists are in the oversight body's hands, yes. But without verification — without the cipher matrix — they're allegations. Circumstantial. Deniable." He paused. "I've been doing this for forty years, Luca. I know exactly how far evidence has to reach before it becomes fact."

Luca crouched, which put him at Orsini's level and made the conversation feel less like a victor addressing a defeated person and more like two professionals discussing a shared problem. "I know," he said. "That's why I'm not here for the case."

Orsini's eyes shifted fractionally.

"The case is Ivan's problem," Luca said. "I'm here for you. Because the cipher verifies the matrix, which verifies the buyer lists, which traces the financial chain back to the authorising signatures on the Sable operation." He held Orsini's gaze. "Including yours. Which makes you the anchor of the evidentiary chain — the person whose testimony, willing or otherwise, connects the allegations to the facts." He paused. "Which is a much more useful thing to have than a glass case."

Orsini was quiet for a moment. He had, Luca thought, the look of a man who had spent forty years being the cleverest person in every room he entered and was doing the specific arithmetic of encountering an exception.

"The oversight process will suppress some of it," Orsini said finally. "The institutional relationships are too embedded."

"Some of it," Luca said. "Not all of it." He straightened. "You spent forty years building a system where the outcome was always controlled. I spent five years playing jazz. The thing I learned about jazz is that you can't control the audience. You can only conduct."

He looked at the man on the floor — at the Maestro reduced to a person in a corridor with his mask off — and felt something he couldn't immediately name. Not satisfaction. Something more like the feeling at the end of a performance, when the room was still and the last note had been played and the whole thing had been exactly what it needed to be.

"Someone will collect you," Luca said. "Stay where you are."

CHAPTER 8
THE CIPHER

THE EXTRACTION TOOK ELEVEN MINUTES.

Luca climbed into the rear of Gabriel's vehicle with Ivan and the glass case and closed the door and let the villa recede behind them. His ribs ached on the right side — Orsini had landed one squarely that he hadn't fully blocked — and he was aware of the specific quality of exhaustion that followed operational work. Not tiredness. Something more structural, as if all the loadbearing elements had been under stress and were now slowly returning to their resting positions.

He had felt this after every operation. He had thought, when he retired, that he would stop feeling it. He had been wrong about that: he had simply gone five years between feelings it, which was different.

Serena was in the passenger seat. She looked back at him once, briefly, and said nothing, which was her version of asking if he was all right.

"I'm fine," he said.

"Your shirt is torn," she said.

"I'm structurally fine."

Maya, in the seat beside him, was examining the glass case with the focused attention she brought to everything that needed to be examined. She had the same quality she'd had during the three days of planning — reading the whole in order to understand the parts, not looking for what she expected but for what was actually there. The Amazon had given her that, Luca suspected. Years of learning that the thing that would kill you was never the thing you'd prepared for specifically.

"The drive is Agency-certified. The codebook is original — the binding matches the era, the ink foxing is real." She looked at Ivan. "The matrix is genuine."

Ivan looked out the window at Naples moving past. "I know," he said.

He had known from the moment he touched the case. He simply hadn't said so until Maya confirmed it, because confirmation from a second person was worth having, and Ivan was not the kind of man who announced things before they were fully established.

They drove in silence for a while. Through the window, the city was doing what cities do at night — the specific, indifferent continuation of ordinary life that always struck Luca as both banal and remarkable after an operation. All these people going about their evenings, unaware that in the hills above them something had just ended.

"Orsini," Gabriel said from the front. "Status."

"Alive and in the corridor," Luca said. "I told him someone would collect him."

"Someone will." Gabriel's voice had the quality of a man making a phone call in his head. "Robert's people have been monitoring the villa since we confirmed the auction. They'll have him inside the hour."

"And then?"

"Then the matrix goes to the oversight body with the buyer lists and the financial chain from the Sable archive. Everything connects. The cipher verifies the provenance. The buyer lists become evidence rather than allegations." Gabriel paused. "As you appear to have told Orsini yourself."

"He was articulate about the problem," Luca said. "I thought it was worth addressing."

"You always think things are worth addressing," Serena said, without heat.

"I'm a conductor. Communication is the whole job."

Maya put the case down between them. "This is the end of the directorate principals thread," she said. "The financial freeze on Voss, the buyer lists from Berlin, the cipher from tonight. Robert's submission has everything it needs."

The end of the directorate principals thread. Luca turned the phrase over. It was not, as Orsini had correctly noted, the end of everything — the institutional relationships were embedded, the process would be slow, some of it would be suppressed. But it was the end of the specific mechanism that had been running since before any of them had retired, the mechanism that had turned their names into entries on a list and their civilian lives into targets.

The thing that Robert had been building toward since he walked out of a Munich archive with a drive in his pocket. The thing that Gabriel had been working through name by name since Lisbon. The thing that Serena had pursued from a Roussillon cottage to a Geneva pavement and that Ivan had opened in a Berlin basement with a key that had waited twenty-five years for him specifically. It had reached its resolution.

"The list," Luca said. "How many names remain?"

Gabriel checked the notebook he kept for exactly this. "After tonight? Twenty-eight."

Twenty-eight people in their lives. Their vineyards and their lock shops and their animal sanctuaries and their university class-rooms. Their morning routines, their regular cafés, their specific patches of ordinary life built carefully over the old ones.

"We keep going," Luca said.

No one disagreed.

CHAPTER 9
MATTEO

THEY MET Matteo at a bar on the waterfront, at midnight, because Matteo had not been at the villa and had therefore not witnessed the extraction and was therefore, until confirmed otherwise, an uncertainty.

He was sitting where Luca had told him to sit, which was evidence of good faith. He was drinking what he always drank, which was a dry Martini that he never finished, because Matteo used drinks as props rather than beverages. He looked, when Luca sat down across from him, like a man who had spent the evening not quite knowing how things had gone.

"The Maestro," Matteo said.

"In custody," Luca said. "The matrix is with the oversight body." He paused. "How did you know about the parallel track?"

Matteo looked at him for a moment. "I've been running for four months. I had a warning from a contact who was connected to the Berlin end of things — she sent me a message about a week after the Locksmith surfaced the Sable archive." He turned his glass. "I knew about the auction through a separate channel. I came to you because you were the closest name on the list I trusted."

"The list," Luca said. "You've seen the list."

"A partial version." Matteo met his eyes. "I know there are other names. People who don't know what's coming."

"We're working through it," Luca said.

Matteo looked out at the harbour. The water was very black and very still, and the lights of the boats on it reflected in long, broken lines. "I'm not like the others," he said. "I never had a civilian life. I've just been running continuously since I left the Agency." He paused. "I don't know how to build what you built. Any of you."

"What does that look like?" Luca asked. "Running continuously."

Matteo was quiet for a moment, in the way of someone who had not been asked that question before and was not sure how to answer it honestly.

"You stop having opinions about things," he said finally. "About places. Food. Whether the weather is good or bad. Everything becomes a function. The café is useful or it isn't. The apartment is secure or it isn't. The person is trustworthy or they aren't." He looked at the Martini. "I was in Lisbon for seven months two years ago. I remember the sightlines and the exit routes. I don't remember anything else about it. I couldn't tell you what the city looked like in the morning."

Luca thought about Lisbon. About Gabriel's classroom and the globes and the specific quality of the October sun on the Alfama rooftops. About a man who had spent fourteen months learning which café charged for the bread basket.

"You remember the operational information," Luca said, "and nothing else."

"Because nothing else was safe to remember." Matteo's voice was even. Not bitter — Luca had expected bitterness and found instead the specific flatness of a person who had made a series of decisions and was describing their consequences. "If you let yourself remember what a city looks like, it becomes a place you might want to return to. And wanting to return to something is—"

"Exposure," Luca said.

"Exposure." Matteo turned his glass once more. "You all chose differently. Built things. Learned things that weren't operationally useful. Became people with histories in a place." He paused. "I couldn't see how to do that without it feeling like a lie."

Luca thought about this. About the specific question of when a cover story became the actual story, and whether the transition was a decision or an accumulation, and what it said about you that you'd let it happen.

"It is a lie," he said. "For a while. And then it isn't." He paused. "The trick is staying in it long enough for the lie to become true. Which requires doing something you're bad at for long enough to get better at it."

Matteo looked at him with an expression that was not quite hope but was the precursor to it. "Is that all there is to it?"

"That's all there is to it." Luca finished his water and stood. "There's a pianist in Palermo who needs an accompanist. He's been advertising the position for three months and no one good has applied. You play the bass, as I recall."

Matteo blinked. "I haven't played in fifteen years."

"Then you'll do it badly for a while," Luca said. "And then you'll do it better."

He left money on the table and walked out into the Naples night, and behind him he heard Matteo not say anything, which was the most promising sound he'd heard all evening.

EPILOGUE: THE FINAL MOVEMENT

THREE WEEKS LATER

THE MORNING LIGHT came through the club's front window at the angle Luca had liked from the first day he'd seen this space — warm, low, hitting the upright bass at exactly the point where the wood was most amber. He'd told the estate agent that this was the determining factor. She had written *"natural lighting"* in her notes and had looked at him with the expression of someone who suspected there was a better reason but was professional enough not to push.

There had been a better reason. There had been several better reasons, including the building's rear exit and the sightline from the first floor to the street and the fact that the basement was dry and structurally sound and accessible through a hatch that most buildings in the quarter didn't have. But the morning light on the bass was genuinely a consideration.

He was sitting at the piano, not playing, just thinking with his hands on the keys the way other people thought with a pen in their hands. The Fazioli was warm under his palms. Outside, Naples was conducting its morning routine: the café across the street, the fishmonger two doors down, the dog that owned the corner by the tabacchi — a big, amber-coloured animal who sat in the same position every morning with the absolute certainty of an animal that knew its territory.

Luca had spent five years building a relationship with this version of the world. The café owner who saved him the last of the almond cornetti because Luca had once, without being asked, helped him carry a delivery up the stairs when the lift was out. The fishmonger who knew Luca didn't eat fish but always saved the good prawns because Luca's neighbour, an elderly woman named Signora Romano, did. The dog, who had decided approximately two years ago that Luca was acceptable, which it communicated by acknowledging his existence without getting up.

This was the life. This was what he had built, not as a cover and not as a performance but as the actual thing — the version of himself that existed when no one was running an operation or threatening a retired assassin or asking him to step back into a role that he had, genuinely, retired from.

He had stepped back into it. He had done so knowing the cost and paying it anyway, and the cost had been two cracked ribs and a torn shirt and four weeks of lying to his band about a bicycle accident.

He did not regret it.

His phone was on the piano lid. It showed a message from Gabriel, sent an hour ago.

Oversight body confirms: Voss remanded pending trial. Three of the directorate principals suspended. Institutional review will take months, but the names are on record. The parallel track is closed.

Below it, a second message from Serena, characteristically shorter.

Good work. Twenty-eight names. Don't stop.

And below that, from Ivan, which surprised him because Ivan rarely messaged:

The Bramah lock. I finished it this morning. Senhora Faria was pleased.

Luca looked at this for a moment and felt something that was not quite the end of a performance but was adjacent to it — the specific quality of a thing that has been built arriving at its completed state. The directorate principals dismantled, the parallel track closed, the cipher verified, Orsini in custody. The work of a year, done.

He thought about Orsini in that corridor, his mask off, doing the arithmetic of a person who had spent forty years being the cleverest person in every room he entered. *You spent forty years building a system where the outcome was always controlled.* He had said it as a diagnosis and Orsini had received it as one. A man who understood control so completely that he'd never learned what to do when the room stopped cooperating.

Luca had spent five years learning what to do when the room stopped cooperating. It was, in fact, the whole lesson of jazz.

The phone showed one more message, arrived while he was looking at the others. A number he didn't recognise — a new burner, the kind you used once and discarded. The message was three lines.

The next name on the list. Female. Former signals intelligence, working as a translator in Helsinki. She doesn't know yet.

She needs contact this week.

—G

Luca looked at it. Then he set the phone face-down on the piano lid and turned his hands over on the keys. Pressed down, not hard enough to sound, just enough to feel the resistance.

The musician's calculation: what does the room need now? What do you give them, and what do you hold back?

The room — this specific room, with the morning light on the bass and the street outside doing its ordinary business — needed nothing from him at this particular moment. The room was fine. The room had been waiting for five years for him to stop treating it like a cover story and he was, finally, letting it be what it was.

A club. In Naples. That he had built from nothing, one decision at a time, the way you built anything that was worth having.

He played the first chord.

Not the opening of anything. Just a chord, held, while the bass caught the light and the street went about its morning and twenty-eight people in their quiet lives went about theirs, not yet knowing what was coming but safer than they'd been yesterday, because the list was in motion and the team was moving and the Conductor was at his piano thinking about Helsinki.

The chord faded.

He played the second one.

Then the third, and by the time the fourth came the thing had become a piece rather than a series of isolated sounds, which was how it always went when you let it — when you stopped controlling and started conducting, giving the room what the room needed rather than what you'd planned to give it.

Outside, the dog at the corner acknowledged his existence without getting up.

Luca kept playing.

Twenty-eight names. One at a time.

The End

Did you enjoy *Retired Assassins' Club, Volume 1*?

Please consider reviewing it on Goodreads, Bookbub or your favorite retailer. Reviews help me reach new readers.

Read **The Archivist**, the next book in the **Retired Assassins' Club** series.

Have you read the FREE prequel, **The traitor**?

ABOUT THE AUTHOR

Sam Chase delivers heart-pounding thrillers crafted for quick reads. Whether you're commuting, relaxing, or need a break, these stories will keep you on the edge of your seat.

Website: www.samchaseauthor.com

Newsletter: samchaseauthor.substack.com

facebook.com/samchaseauthor

x.com/samchaseauthor

amazon.com/author/samchasemystery

bookbub.com/authors/sam-chase-0987d23f-73d9-4b97-9954-5f9fce0c0ce3

goodreads.com/samchaseauthor

ALSO BY SAM CHASE

Retired Assassins' Club

The Scholar

The Widow

The Ghost

The Locksmith

The Conductor

Agents of Deception

Alliance

Shadow Pursuit

Double Crossed

Deep Cover

Endgame

City of Lies

Hunted

Fractured

Veiled

Marked

Exposed

The Man at the Window

Across the Street

Behind the Glass

Inside the Door

Under the Floor

Beyond the Yrad

www.ingramcontent.com/pod-product-compliance
Lightning Source LLC
Chambersburg PA
CBHW020328260626
47156CB00004B/1434